The Last Single
Girl

Bria Quinlan

BREW HA HA SERIES

It's in His Kiss
The Last Single Girl
Worth the Fall
The Catching Kind

BREW AFTER DARK Shorts
Love in Tune
Sweet As Cake

~*~

YA Books by Bria Quinlan

Secret Girlfriend (RVHS #1)
Secret Life (RVHS #2)
Wreckless

ONE

DATING TRUTH #1: Just when you've comfortably established a group of single girlfriends, disaster strikes.

J ONATHAN IS EVERYTHING I EVER wanted in a guy." Angie spun the cocktail stirrer around her martini. "I can't believe my brother never brought him home before. I mean, they've been best friends since college."

She said it as if *college* was decades ago instead of only a couple years. I couldn't help but wonder if maybe knowing his sister would steal his best friend was why he'd never brought Jonathan home. He'd been hiding the poor guy. Caving meant he'd probably lost him forever.

"Wow." Claire grinned. It made me nervous.

It wasn't that she didn't like Angie. But Claire's sense of humor was cutting, even if it was right on. She had the wardrobe of Carrie Bradshaw and the wit of Dorothy Parker. Her commentary always felt like it came out of nowhere. Like

1

a summer cold. One day you're at the beach, then—Bam!—you're sick in bed. She kind of scared me.

"Going home must be the way to find a guy," Claire continued before a drama-pause. "I got back together with Marcus."

"Really?" Becca pushed her drink out of her way. "How did that happen?"

Not surprisingly, I was lost. "Who's Marcus?"

Claire waved down the waitress and pointed to her half-full drink, not bothering to look my way. "I always forget you weren't around for that."

The truth was, I wasn't around for a lot of things with these ladies.

Last fall I'd had a lovely group of girlfriends. Just like any group, you had an inner circle of friends and loosely touching outer circles. Like a Venn diagram of relationships. A comfy little life with plenty of friends to go around.

Until the first engagements...then weddings...then houses in the suburbs happened. Next thing you know, your inner circle is married and there you are. Left with a mish-mash of looser, less cohesive circles. Still a nice little group though. Life was good.

Until Thanksgiving week.

"Marcus and I grew up together, but didn't start dating until senior year of college. When we graduated, he moved back to run the family's construction company and I moved here to go into advertising. Can you see *me* living in the Great American Farmland?"

No. I really couldn't. Claire refused to let anyone without local celebrity status touch her hair or skin. Just staying groomed would mean monthly four-hour drives.

"But when I saw him at the football game Thursday, it was like we'd never been apart and…Well, let's just say everything is back on track."

She sounded so happy—so *not* Claire—I didn't have the heart to ask how it was going to work out this time around.

"I can't believe you guys hooked up over the weekend, because"—Becca drew the word out and I knew what was coming—"I met the greatest guy on the plane. He's a lawyer in New York. We sat next to each other. I've never been so happy to be stuck on the tarmac for three hours. He changed his flight so we did part of our return together too. And,"—Becca sucked in an excited breath before finishing in a rush—"he's coming here for New Year's."

I sat back listening to them gush about their guys—new and recycled—and their trips and the New Year and how great the holiday was going to be.

"You know what we should do? If they're all coming here, we should change our reservation for New Year's."

Wait. What? *No.*

"We'll just add them to our table."

"But I thought it was sold out." I tried to keep the desperation out of my voice. We'd planned this months ago. The single girls having a fun night out. No couples making us feel all single-loserish on the second biggest date night of the year.

"I'll call my ticket guy right now. I'm sure he can hook us up." Claire was on her phone before I could say *girls' night.* "Hi, handsome. It's Claire. I'm looking for a favor." She laughed her that's-not-funny-but-I-need-something-from-you laugh before flashing our table a grin. "Oh, you're too sweet…I know, right? I need a little help with our table for the Murder on the Rocks party...I know, right? I'm going to look fabulous in my flapper dress. The whole roaring twenties murder mystery is genius."

Angie and Becca both pushed their drinks aside to lean in, listening over the rumble of the growing bar crowd.

"Well, we'd like to get a few more people seated with us. Is there anyway we could shuffle them in?...Uh-huh...Yup... Absolutely. I can make sure you get on the list for that opening...Of course. Well, we need three more."

"Wait." Angie waved her hand in front of Clair. "What about Sarah?"

Everyone turned my way and I was tempted to tell them I was engaged and getting married on New Year's Eve if they and their newly found plus-ones were available.

"Oh. Sarah, did you meet someone too?" Since the beginning of time—otherwise known as Julie's wedding four years ago—Claire disliked me on sight. Her competitive nature seemed to triple around me. Only I didn't really know what we were competing over, so I just tried to stay out of her way.

I thought about lying, but knew faking a boyfriend would lead to all kinds of social pitfalls I couldn't navigate. Plus, I'd seen *The Wedding Date*. That was *so* a path I didn't want to walk down.

"No. Not really." I dragged the *really* out hoping they'd read something into it I didn't mean—like maybe there was a guy I'd been holding out on them about. An amazingly hot guy who owned a small, undisclosed island off the coast of a certain wealthy country. *Obviously* I couldn't talk about him for security reasons.

"Say four," Angie whispered. "I'm sure Sarah won't have a problem getting a date."

Claire cocked an eyebrow at me as if she not only knew how doubtful it was, but she expected me to back her up. *Oh, no, Claire. Don't ask for a fourth seat. We all know no one would ever want to go out with me, let alone give up one of the best party nights of the year to hang out with a nerdy museum curator.*

Right.

Instead, I just smiled.

And thought nasty thoughts.

Claire tilted her head as if she could read my mind and smiled in a way that clearly said, *Oh. You poor thing.*

"Why don't you make it four? That's a full table, right?" Claire grinned and nodded. "Just put it on my credit card. We'll take care of splitting it on our end."

Great. Way to kick yourself in the rear, Sarah. Exactly what makes the holidays shiny. Paying for an empty chair.

TWO

DATING TRUTH #2: No man will ever understand and love you like your best friend does.

T HIS IS JANE. I'M EITHER *lugging around my beautiful daughter or hanging out with my gorgeous husband. Or I'm lying and cleaning the toilets. Either way, leave a message after the beep."*

BEEP.

"Hey Jane. It's Sarah. Just calling to chat. Hope your Thanksgiving was great. Give me a ring." I paused, about to hang up, then rushed on before I could cave. "Also, I'm emailing you something right now. If you could look at it, not show Matt, and not tell anyone, that would be great. Okaythanksbye."

I hurried through the last words, hanging up before I could change my mind.

I was feeling panicked. I knew this happened. Knew someone had to have the *honor*. But I never thought I might be *the last single girl*.

It felt like a title.

Maybe I should have business cards made.

Or…maybe not.

It wasn't just the idea of being the last single girl. It was everything that went with it. The things you weren't invited to because people thought you'd be uncomfortable alone. The way Certain Women always reminded you they had someone…and you didn't. The feeling of loneliness you sometimes felt, even with your best friend because you knew you were no longer *her* best friend.

And so, like any emotionally cornered woman, I did something extreme.

I joined eLove.com to try to find someone special—or not horrible—for New Year's.

The internet had found me everything else of import over the last few years: An apartment, a job, a car…that Kate Spade bag. So, yes, I had some confidence in the internet.

But as I glanced over my ad, I knew there was no way around it. Jane was going to have to be my voice of reason. Every time I reread it, all I could think was any sane person would assume a golden retriever puppy was looking for a date.

I'd actually said I liked sunny days and enjoyed a nice hike before curling up in front of my fireplace for a cozy night in.

Why didn't I just add a picture of my favorite chew toy?

Of course, I was a golden retriever with very expensive shoes and a condo in town, but still.

7

I hit send and tried to pretend my best friend wasn't somewhere looking at her iPhone and laughing hysterically.

It took a lot more effort than I wanted to admit.

While I waited to hear back, I did what any logical woman would do—I went to the library and got every book on dating written in the last four years.

Yes, I used the self-checkout line.

I skimmed through them all, glancing at 'rules' and making notes about profiles. I created lists of what were Must Haves and No Ways and then crossed half of them off after every book added you couldn't be too picky.

Most of the books had dual personalities like that.

Part of me wanted to ignore the phone when Jane's ringtone sounded. She'd gotten back to me about four hours faster than expected. Obviously my message—or personal ad—warranted a fairly immediate phone call. That couldn't be a good sign.

I hit the answer button and started before she could. "If you laugh, I'm hanging up, moving out of state, and you'll never see me again."

"I'm not laughing. I've been married less than two years. I remember how much it stunk trying to find the right guy."

I knew she did. She never pulled any of that married crap. That, *Oh, just wait and the right guy will show up* OR *If you just did fill-in-the-blank you wouldn't be living your life alone.*

"Honestly, I'm glad you sent it to me. I made a bunch of changes." Jane made a soft cooing sound. I could only assume it was for the baby. Although, if I were being honest, it *was* an oddly reassuring noise. "Who knows you better than I do, right? I may be partial, but I love you and I'll kick

8

anyone's rear-end who doesn't appreciate you the way he should."

My eyes teared up. I held the phone away from my head and sniffed, not wanting her to know how much her words affected me.

"I just sent it. You should get it in a second." More cooing, then a soft splash. "I'm giving Dahlia her bath. Or she's giving me a bath, one or the other. Tell me, why the sudden urge to e-date?"

I didn't want to own up to my impending spinsterhood, but she probably saw it coming anyway. I filled her in on our New Year's plans and how everyone magically came home from Thanksgiving weekend with a boyfriend. How girls' night out had become the third—make that seventh—wheel fiasco.

"So, The Alphabet just changed all your plans and expected you to hang with them and their new boyfriends?"

Jane had been calling them The Alphabet since before she'd gotten married. The three of them—Angie, Becca, and Claire—had known each other the longest. As the single girls fell to the wayside, Claire had scooped up her compatriots and made herself Alpha-something-else-that-starts-with-B.

I think they'd been surprised to find me among their ranks. Maybe if my name had been Deirdre....

"Yup. Claire got four seats added to our table."

"I never liked her." Jane was, among other things, fiercely loyal. "And it's not just that she treats you like an afterthought. She's never kind to anyone. Kittens couldn't melt her."

"Well, the girl has connections. There's no party she can't get us into."

"Right. Because you've always been such a party girl. I know how those museum curators are. Crazier than rock stars."

"You totally underestimate the rock star'ness of some of my sistren."

"Why don't you just come here? You know you're always welcome. You don't need a guy to get into my house."

The best part of the statement was I knew she meant it. It wasn't a pity thing, or a—*because-we're-friends-I-have-to-say-this*—thing.

"I know. And thanks. But I have to have a life outside the museum, and occasionally visiting you and Michelle." I choked back the rest of the words about how I was starting to feel left behind and how I was afraid of being alone—not just with no boyfriend, but with no free girlfriends.

"There's no sense in being miserable on New Year's just to prove you can. We're having a game night. Michelle and Roger are coming over. Our new neighbors Mitch and Emily will be here. We hired a neighborhood girl to babysit."

"Wow, you got a babysitter?" That involved letting Dahlia out of her line of vision.

"Um. Well, yes." Jane made a small coughing noise.

"What was that?"

"I said…she's going to babysit in the back room."

"Jane, if I didn't love you, I wouldn't bother to tell you you're one *TIME Magazine* cover away from being *that* Mom."

She laughed, which was good. Even as we built different lives, we still *got* each other.

"Sarah, she's four months, not four years. I'm getting better. I let Matt's mother take her the other day and didn't even call to check in—even when she was ten minutes late. I'm sure she did it on purpose. You know that *woman* doesn't like me."

See? Right there? A reason it was better to be single. Mothers-in-law.

"I think I'll try Plan A first."

"You only have four weeks till New Year's. How are you going—Dahlia. No. Don't drink that. That's shampoo. Yucky."

I laughed as the splashing got louder. When Jane had first had the baby, we'd have hung up and hoped to talk later. But over the last few months we'd learned better.

"Sorry about that. So, the plan?"

"I'm going to narrow it down to my top five guys in the first week. I'll spend the second week getting to know them. Then the few days before and after Christmas I'll do meet-ups and see how it goes. That gives me a little squishy room before New Year's."

This met with silence. Even the splashing had magically stopped.

"Well, see what you think of my notes. Also, I expect you to send me your username and password so I can check these guys out." Jane sucked in a breath. I could picture her working up the nerve to say something. "You know it doesn't matter if you're dating someone or not. That was girls' night. If they screw it up, that's not on you."

I shouldn't have needed to hear that so badly, but all the same....

"Thanks. Really. Thanks."

"Don't forget...username and password."

"As long as you don't start masquerading as me."

"I make no promise."

Of course she didn't.

THREE

Downtown Doctor – I work at a large medical center downtown. It takes a lot of my time, but I'm looking for someone to share those other moments with. Someone who enjoys museums, movies, music, and a good meal. I'd love to find an independent woman who still lets me spoil her a little.

DOWNTOWN DOCTOR—OR TREY—WAS scheduled to meet me at one-thirty. We'd been emailing almost since the beginning. Obviously, he had me at *museum*, but I was looking forward to seeing if that spark was there. From his profile, he was exactly my type: Tall, good looking, successful. He understood having a career that was not only very involving, but a passion.

On Jane's command, we were meeting at a neutral location—a coffee shop I'd found online.

The cafe was about half a block away from the train, tucked down a side street. At the sight of it, I sucked in a little breath. It was the most magical looking coffee shop ever.

It was as if someone had taken an Irish cottage and set it down among the taller brownstones of the neighborhood. Green shutters stretched out around black framed windows, and gas lamps flickered on each side of the entry.

Talk about romantic meeting places.

I pushed through the heavy oak door and stopped, surprised to see the inside matched the outside. Instead of ugly wooden IKEA chairs and sterile metal and wood tables, cozy looking mix-and-match chairs nestled under oak tables of different sizes and shapes. At the far end of the room, a fireplace crackled away, framed by floor-to-ceiling bookcases. Several stuffed chairs and a heavy looking coffee table cornered them off.

But the best part was the art.

An obviously well planned collection graced one wall, but the exhibit itself needed work.

All the right information was there, but the lighting was off and the placards poorly placed. The work would never sell like that, no matter how talented the artist.

"Do you like it?" The deep voice rumbled behind me, not at all what I expected in such a quaint setting.

Hopefully it was Trey because there was no way anything less than hot could be connected to a voice like that. I turned, expecting to see perfectly polished, six-foot-two, suited professional hotness. That wasn't what I met at all and I was seriously beginning to question eLove's search engine capabilities and men's profiles.

He wasn't hot. And he wasn't tall. He definitely wasn't polished. To be fair, he was taller than me at five-ten, but I like my men *towering*. And I guess he was good looking in an approachable way. Lean with wide shoulders where I liked my men built. But his hair…His hair made me want to smooth it down—too long to tame, too short to lay flat.

This had definitely better not be Trey.

"The artist obviously has a lot of skill. I like the series. Cathedral naves? Not a lot of people would think to paint such a small detail from such a large space."

"I know. That's what drew me to it. It's very…safe feeling, right?" He stared at the paintings a bit longer before turning his warm brown eyes on me. "I'm John."

I took his offered hand, trying to be polite while I moved things along. I suspected hanging out with some random guy when your date came in was not the best first impression.

"Sarah."

"Welcome to The Brew Ha Ha, Sarah. First time in?"

"Um, yes?" It seemed odd to share that with someone, especially someone I didn't know.

"Great. I bought the place about four months ago. I'm still getting to know the regulars. Can I get you something?"

Oh. The owner. Less weird then.

"I'm meeting someone, but sure." I followed him to the counter and looked over the menu. It was oddly comforting to see the sizes small, medium and large. I wasn't a fan of coffee guess work. After ordering a medium chai tea, I headed back to the art wall.

It was quiet, only one older gentleman sitting in the corner reading a newspaper. I knew that couldn't be great for business, but it was perfect for me.

"You really seem to like the gallery."

"Exhibit. Or showing. Or even display."

"I'm sorry, what?"

"That's what you call the display, not a gallery. That's something else."

"Oh." John smiled a funny little smile. He seemed more confused by my correcting him than by the word.

"Sorry. It's just…I work in a museum. This is part of what I do."

I didn't tell him how poorly planned his display was.

"That must be really interesting. This is my first time having anything on the walls. I mean, besides the bad prints that were here before. I'm trying to bring in some more clientele."

"I like it like this." The voice came from the far side of the room. "Nice and *quiet*."

"That's Ernest." John lowered his voice. "Don't mind him. His hobby is being grumpy."

"Oh." I mean, what else could you really say to that?

"I'll let you relax before your friend gets here. If you need anything, let me know."

John gave me a grin and headed back toward the counter, pulling a towel off a table as he went.

I settled in one of the overstuffed chairs near the fireplace, enjoying the space. I was checking my emails—a weekend hazard when you worked for a museum—when a tall man who was even better looking than the picture of him at his sister's wedding rushed in the door.

"Sarah? I'm so sorry I'm late."

I glanced at the clock over the counter. He was two minutes late—if the clock wasn't fast.

I rose and stuck my hand out, unsure of etiquette for eLove meet-ups.

"Hi. It's nice to meet you. You're not late at all." I smiled, trying to go for reassuring, when really I was just feeling nervous.

"Really?" He glanced at his watch and sort of frowned. In his world two minutes must have been an eternity.

Good to know.

"Can I get you a refill?"

I hefted my half-full tea and shook my head. "No thanks. I just got this."

"I'll be right back." He smiled. It was a reassuring smile. One I was sure he used in the hospital all the time. It made me wonder how used to handling people he was. If he was handling me.

Stop. Just stop.

Jane had warned me not to jump to the worst assumptions right away. She said, let things play out and not read into everything.

She also said she wanted immediate text updates as soon as he left. He was so good looking I wanted to pre-date text her.

Trey paid for his drink and gave John a curt nod to end their conversation. He wandered across the café, glancing at all the hominess.

"Cute place. Do you come here often?" As soon as the words left his mouth he blushed. And just like that I relaxed. "I mean, is this a regular hangout?"

"It is really cute, isn't it? And nope, this is my first time here. I thought somewhere neither of us would feel like we might run into people would be comfortable."

"You put a lot of thought into this?"

"To be honest, this is my first time online dating. My girlfriends had a lot to say about it. Lots of so-called *rules*."

"Like what?"

"Oh, you know. Be on time, but that's just manners. Coffee, not dinner. Somewhere not too close to home. Don't get in anyone's car." I shrugged. "Most of them were just common sense."

"Any really odd ones?"

I almost hated to tell him, but why not find out if he had a sense of humor?

"Michelle suggested getting close enough to smell you. If you smelled like a pet, then your house would reek of animals and if we got married I'd be stuck in a dog-scented house for the rest of my life and probably even win it in the divorce. She's such an optimist. I told her let's see if we make it through coffee."

He laughed—a deep-chested sound. Obviously weird smells and marriage in the first five minutes wasn't going to scare him off.

"I don't have pets. I'd love to have a dog, but my hours are a little crazy. I don't think it would be fair to him to be stuck in the house all day. How about you?"

"Well, there's Winston. But he's just a beta fish, so he's stuck in the house all day either way."

Look at me being all charming and stuff.

"So, Trey, tell me about your job." I ran through all the directions in the dating books. Ask about him, smile, lean in, look interested even if you're not.

Although, let's be honest. A good-looking, successful doctor starts telling you how he enjoys his practice as a primary care physician and spending his vacation time hiking in Europe, it's pretty easy to look interested.

Every time I tried to follow up, he'd jump in with something like *Sarah, where has your favorite trip been* or *I know you work in a museum, does that mean you don't enjoying going to them anymore?*

"Why exactly are you online dating?" I'd been wanting to ask since he'd whistled—a pre-email move—at me online. No one could be this good, could he?

"I work with doctors and nurses all day. I know the kind of schedule and pressures we have." He shrugged as if it just couldn't be helped. "I know I'd never be able to make it work with someone just like me. I wanted to meet someone outside that world. Someone a bit...softer. I know. That sounds horrible. I'm not a monster or anything. Just too focused. My best friend told me I need to meet someone who knows how to help me leave it at work."

I could understand that. Everyone needed balance. My last boyfriend didn't understand that being a curator meant I was often at the museum for special events...even at night, even on the weekends.

"What about you? Why online dating?"

Because I was desperate for a New Year's date just didn't seem to have the same ring to it.

"Well, most of my close friends are married, so my social life often revolves around places you don't meet other singles. I'm not looking to end up at the altar tomorrow, but I realized all the places I used to meet interesting men were places you can't go alone. And you also can't bring a pregnant woman with a stroller."

"Like *Sweet Home Alabama*."

He did *not* just reference my favorite movie.

"You have a baby," he continued, "in a bar."

"Exactly. Although I'm a little surprised by your ability to quote chick flicks."

"My last girlfriend loved movies. All we did was stay in and watch rom coms."

"Oh." Yeah, not the life I envisioned for myself.

"Exactly. You can see why it didn't work out. Even getting her to try a new restaurant was like pulling teeth."

We chatted for almost three hours—or two chai tea refills—before I realized the time.

I'd expected him to stay an hour tops. There was no way I'd thought my first date would be it—would be the guy I not only wanted to spend New Year's with, but maybe a whole bunch of time after that. He was exactly what I'd always been looking for. We totally matched.

Unfortunately, I'd planned to meet someone else that afternoon. Both men had said it was their only day free for the next few weeks, so I'd said yes to both.

I was trying to figure out a nice way to end the date, when I heard, "Trey. What's up?"

I glanced up and panicked.

The table was too small. I'd never be able to hide under it. The bathroom? Too far away.

FOUR

Rock Guy—I like to climb stuff—and I don't mean just the corporate ladder. In my free time I rock climb locally as well as a guided climb trip each summer. I'm looking for someone to share that sense of wonder and adventure with and bring it into everyday life.

I GLANCED OVER MY SHOULDER to find a good-looking man in a blue pullover smiling down at us. One who looked suspiciously like Date Two's profile picture.

"Hey, man." Trey stood and shook the guy's hand, doing that half-hug thing men do instead of just showing affection. "What are you doing here?"

"I'm meeting someone."

"Weird." Trey turned to me, offering his hand as I stood. "This is Sarah."

"Sarah?" It was the way he said my name that told me we were all going downhill from there. "Sarah, Art Girl, Sarah?"

"Oh. Yeah." I should have known my perfect date would get not-so-perfect at some point. But hey...as Jane always joked, it was a story we could tell our grandkids. "Adam?"

Trey waved a hand between us. "How do you guys know each other?"

"We don't. I mean, we do, but we don't. Adam and I were matched up on eLove too." This shouldn't feel so awkward. "You were so busy and interesting and stuff, I figured we'd get together and then you'd be off to do something. So, when Adam said he could only meet up tonight, it seemed like a good idea."

Both guys looked at me. Maybe less would have been more in that explanation.

"Oh." Trey studied me, disappointment coming through as his brows drew together. "So..."

"So?" I wasn't sure what he wanted to say. All I knew was I'd just been on one the best dates of my life and I was really hoping it wasn't going to end awkwardly.

"So, Adam's my best friend. High school. College roommates. Travel buddies."

"Oh." Okay. Adam's date was going to go down as the shortest one in the history of mankind. Basically ending when he said hello.

"We've made a deal we'd..." Trey looked at Adam who only raised an eyebrow at him. "We don't date the same girls."

So, Adam's one-second date would have to be struck from the dating history of Sarah Joy Gable. I was okay with that.

"Okay." I got it. Never come between friends. It was good to see guys who had been that close for so long. It said a lot of good things about Trey.

22

"So, I'm going to have to cancel our plans for next week." He took my hand and smiled down at me; that reassuring smile I'm sure he used all the time at work. "You understand, right?"

"Um, no?" We'd had a great date. It went three times longer than expected with nothing but good vibes and, because I'd chatted with his best friend, we were off?

"Adam's been one of the few friends I've been able to keep through all the crazy school and residency and work stuff. We can't go out with the same girl. And since you guys have been chatting, we'd never make anyone pick. It would just get...awkward."

As compared to this. This wasn't awkward at all—unless you were, you know, *human*.

"So. That's it then." I tried not to let the last word drift into a question. Trey was being pretty clear.

"I'm sorry. It was *great* to meet you. I hope I meet someone just like you soon."

Great. I was being tossed over for someone he *might* someday meet just like me.

"You too." Seriously. Someone just like him. Only without the best guy friend who couldn't compromise.

Trey shook his head one time and headed toward the door. Adam just looked down at me like I'd done something horrible on purpose. "Nice to meet you."

"Uh, you too?"

He joined Trey at the door, giving him a slap on the back before they headed out into the already dark late-afternoon.

FIVE

DATING TRUTH #3: My mama always told me, dating was like a box of Crayons. Wait. What?

I STOOD AT THE TABLE, watching the closed door and wondering if I was on one of those weird MTV shows. I should have guessed three hours ago it was a set up. No guy could really be that perfect, right?

"Sarah?" John called me from behind the counter. "Everything okay?"

No. No it wasn't.

I fell into my chair and stared at my tea.

The scrape of wood on wood had me glancing up to watch John join me.

"The date looked like it went pretty well." John pushed a fresh pot of tea my way.

Teapots. Charming.

"Yeah. It was pretty much perfect." I poured us each a cup of tea, watching the amber liquid splash about in the shallow white porcelain. "How'd you know it was a date?"

"I run a café. They're like the number one spot for first dates." He lifted his glass, smiling at me over the rim. "Why don't you tell me why you're staring at the door and looking a bit disappointed then?"

I didn't really want to have this conversation. I was still working to rewrite the positive text messages I'd been composing in my head during the date. Instead of *Jane! Met the man of my dreams—can't wait for you to meet him!* I was now dealing with, *Met the man of my dreams. After one date he threw me over for his best friend.*

Not very complimentary.

Jane, of course, would make a completely inappropriate comment about him secretly being gay. Which I would know was wrong and unfair on a lot of levels, but would still make me feel a bit better.

"Come on now." John pulled his chair in and set his elbows on the table. "I'm basically the sober version of a bartender. You'd be shocked what people tell me."

Why not? Texting could be tedious anyway.

"Okay." I sipped at the tea and totally got derailed. "Wow, what is this?"

"Chamomile with lemon grass and a bit of ginger."

"It's soothing with a bit of a kick."

"That's the point. I'm still working on just how much ginger is enough, but not too much."

"You made this?"

"Yup. I've started blending the teas. I'd like to start measuring them out for sale."

25

Brilliant.

Between that and the new art, John was really adding some nice touches to his venture.

"Anyway, what prompted sadness after a great date?"

"Right. So, that was Trey...I should back up." Might as well. I was going to be seeing a lot of John over the next two weeks. "I had plans for a girls' night on New Year's with the dregs of the single girlfriends. And they all came back from Thanksgiving with boyfriends."

John nodded. It wasn't like it was a surprise where this was heading.

"Next thing you know, I'm the seventh wheel on girls' night, which is now new couple's night."

"So, you thought you'd find a date online."

It had been more than that I realized. I wasn't sure how much I wanted to tell John—even if he was my sober bartender.

Realizing I was suddenly the *last* single girl...it had been a little depressing.

"I have almost three more weeks till New Year's. I thought I'd be able to post my profile and get to know a couple guys online the first week, spend the middle two weeks getting to know each one, and then have a week buffer hoping one might come with me to the Murder Mystery Dinner thing."

"Makes sense." John poured a bit more tea and waited for me to continue. When I didn't, he asked, "So, how'd the first date go?"

I sucked in a deep breath trying not to sound let down. "That was actually dates one and two. Date One went great. We really hit it off. Date Two got here, ended up being Date

One's best friend, and they went with some childhood pact to never fight over a girl, and left."

"Wait, they left even though you technically hadn't met Date Two yet?"

"Yup."

"Date One went really well and he just left because you'd emailed his best friend a few times?"

"We'd emailed once and he said with the holidays being so busy we should just meet up."

"So, you'd gotten one email from him? I spend more time emailing people to unsubscribe from those annoying marketing emails."

I snorted tea out my nose. It wasn't pretty, but it just made me laugh harder.

"Date One is showing a severe lack of intelligence. He's going to be single forever."

"He's a really nice guy."

"That doesn't make him any less stupid."

"Actually, he's a doctor."

"A stupid doctor." John shook his head. "On the upside, if your first date—"

"First *two* dates."

"—was that good, that means you'll be finding the right guy. Now that you're out there putting your mind to it. I'm sure you can do anything you put your mind to."

"Oh, thanks." That was really sweet.

"How many dates have you scheduled?"

"Five."

"Nice. Like one of those Crayon starter boxes you get when you're a kid. You'll have a whole rainbow thing going on."

I'd settle for just one right hue—I mean, guy. Or a guy named Hugh.

"Have you ever done online dating?" I asked. They say most people had, right?

"No."

Or not.

"Okay." I wasn't sure what else to say short of *How 'bout those Pats?*

After a moment John the-sober-bartender added, "I was actually in a pretty long-term relationship until a few months ago."

Again. Oh.

"I'm sorry?" I wasn't sure if I was supposed to be sorry or not. I hated blind conversations like this.

"No. It's okay. She didn't like how much time starting my own business took. Also, she said she hadn't signed on for this."

"For a coffee shop?" Who ever really assumes they've signed on for a coffee shop?

"For me not making a lot of money. Coffee shop startups aren't exactly raking in the dough. This one is barely cutting even." John winked at me and smiled before adding, "I'm lucky I get a lot of neighborhood walk-through business in the morning. Commuters catching the train."

"It's good to have a niche. So, what *had* she signed on for?"

"I was in finance."

"A lot of people are."

"No, I mean, I was fast-tracked. They expected me to be sitting in an executive office by the time I was forty."

Wow. Over achiever much? That made my career drive look lazy.

"But that's not what you wanted?"

"I thought it was. And then one night I met some friends for dinner. I hadn't seen them in almost a year. They were talking about the movies they'd seen, the books they were reading, the concerts they had tickets too. And then I realized I was thirty and working eighty-hours a week and missing my life."

"That's a lot to realize during one dinner."

"Tell me about it." John sipped at his tea slowly, as if he were stalling the story out or reconsidering it in his head. "I called in sick the next day. I thought they were going to send an ambulance to my house. I'd crawled in to work near death before and I couldn't get the admin to believe I wasn't dying. But how do you say, I just need a day away from all of you?"

"Most of us say it just like that."

He laughed, snorting a little of the tea he sipped. "Right. Now I know that. Anyway, I went for a walk and found this place. It looked exactly like the kind of place I should have been hanging out at on Saturday mornings. Drinking my coffee, reading my paper, maybe a dog tied under my table outside. I came in and the owner, Fredrick, joined me. We got to talking. One thing led to another and here we are. You know."

Um. No.

"How exactly does one thing lead to another to owning a coffee shop?"

"Fredrick told me he was selling. We joked about me buying it. I went back to work the next day, but I couldn't stop thinking about it. I did what finance guys do, I ran the numbers. I called him and asked him to fax his financials. I ran more numbers. I wrote up a plan that weekend, got the loan, bought the place and quit my job."

"Wow."

"Right? Only, I'd tried to talk to Sheila about it and she kept dismissing it. She thought it was a whim. Like how we always said we should go to St Maarten. But it wasn't. Then, when my hours grew while my paycheck shrunk, she got really confused."

Made sense. The power couple suddenly unbalance. The woman not sure what to do with all the changes. I could understand how that would be a lot to take in.

"How long did she last?"

"Less than a month. And of course that was the worst time. The two months before I opened and the first after opening were all trial and error." He leaned his head against the headrest and closed his eyes. "Looking back, it's horrible to say, but I was maybe a little relieved when she called it quits. It was too much trying to balance all the new startup and her suddenly wanting my attention. It wasn't like I'd had tons of free time before The Brew."

Whoever this Shelia person was, I didn't think I liked her.

"So, no," he continued. "I haven't tried online dating. I think I'll give it the old-fashioned try first."

Before I could ask what that meant, he was clearing the tray away and heading for the counter.

Maybe the holidays would bring us both what we wanted.

SIX

Suit & Tie Plus — My life is pretty full. I'm blessed with lots of little joys. Looking for someone who enjoys quiet nights at home and is good at saying what's on her mind. No cream puffs. I want a woman who knows what she wants and is good at drawing boundaries.

H EY, SARAH!" JOHN WAVED FROM the counter where he put together Ernest's tea tray.

I waved back as I wandered over to the comfy seats by the fire, tossed my jacket over the back of one and set my bag down. The art wall was still pulling my attention. My fingers itched to lower the paintings about an inch and a half. It was invaluable. Everyone hung their walling décor too high.

"You're eyeing my art again." John had snuck up to look over my shoulder.

"I am."

"I've been playing with it. Shifting some things around. I sold one for him."

"That's great. He's really talented."

"So, what time is Date Three going to be here?"

"In about thirty minutes." I turned to face him before I could ask for a ladder and toolbox. "How's Ernest?"

"Still grumpy. But as my one regular, he's allowed."

"A few more dates and you'll be able to call me a regular too."

"Here's hoping." He shoved his hand through his hair and out of his eyes. "Can I get you something?"

"Have you been playing with any more teas?"

"Today's special practice blend is green tea with chipped coconut."

"Great. I'll try that." I followed him to the counter and watched him measure leafy things into a small bag before tying it off.

I pulled out my wallet and dug around for a five. One of the reasons I'd been getting to the café before my dates was to buy my own drinks. It felt weird to go through the whole who-buys-what thing while I was date shopping.

"Put your wallet away. You're my guinea pig."

While that was really sweet, watching him struggle to get this café moving meant I couldn't imagine taking my tea for free.

"John, I can't expect you to give me tea every time I'm here."

"Trust me. With some of my practice blends you'll be thinking I should pay you."

As he turned around to put the tea tray together, I glanced for the tip jar. When I didn't find one, I leaned over the counter and slipped the five under the register's keyboard.

"Here you go. Good luck with Date Three."

"Thanks." He really was sweet. Plus, The Brew Ha Ha was exactly the type of place people liked to come in and feel at home in. It had to gain traction soon.

I set the tray on the coffee table and settled back to wait. I spent the time reviewing Date Three's profile for things to discuss.

It was almost seven when a haggard looking man attempting to corral three children rushed in. He brought the kids to the counter and let them each pick out a treat. While they did, he glanced around the café, his gaze landing on me.

He looked oddly familiar. Maybe the family who lived upstairs from me? I dismissed the idea as soon as I'd considered it. If this was the upstairs family, I'd have moved out already. The boys alone made enough noise for four families.

They settled at the far end of the café at a collection of tables. The man pulled out a bunch of games and coloring books and leaned in to give them what looked like a stern lecture.

Instead of sitting down, he turned and strode across the café. Stopping in front of me. Oh, lord. No, please.

"Sarah?" Date Three had a nice voice, was good looking, and seemed to be struggling not to look frazzled.

"Malcolm?" I was still hoping I was wrong. That the oddly familiar face wasn't from his profile pics.

But at his name, he seemed to relax.

"It's nice to meet you." He stuck his hand out and waited while I stood and shook it. "Sorry about the kids. My sitter canceled at the last minute and since we didn't swap phone numbers I wasn't really sure what to do."

I almost told him ninety percent of people under sixty had a smartphone so an email would have done it. But I could see he was really working to make this as *not* awkward as possible.

Malcolm had been very sweet in his emails. He hadn't mentioned his kids, which seemed like a huge oversight. I understood a lot of women might shy away from giving a guy with kids a chance, but wouldn't you want to know that ahead of time? But what were you going to do? I could go with it.

He set his coffee down and settled into the chair next to me, pushing it a bit so he was only halfway facing me.

"So, this is great. Nice coffee shop. I've never been here before."

"Thanks. All I did was pick it. John, the owner, is the secret behind the magic." I followed Malcolm's gaze toward his kids. "So, do you—"

"Jeffery." Malcolm half stood, pointing toward the table where his kids sat. "Put that down. You brought your own coloring books."

Jeffery looked like he was going to ignore the commandment, hugging the coloring book to his chest.

"You also have your Gameboy. That's going to have to be how you spend your time. Now hand her back her book."

The little girl next to him with a blue crayon gripped in her hand held out her free hand with a dignity you expected from a queen. Jeffery tossed the coloring book down in front of her and picked up his game.

"Sorry about that. You wouldn't believe how hard it is to find a babysitter."

"No problem. Kids can be a handful."

"Do you have any kids?"

Seriously? I almost told him if I'd had kids they would have been mentioned in my profile. You know, that page with all your *important* information?

"No. No kids."

"Have you been married before?"

Again. Profile page.

Come to think of it, I didn't think I picked anyone who had been divorced. I remembered thinking anyone who was divorced at my age was probably in a different place than I was. Maybe later, but it just seemed so foreign an idea at twenty-nine.

"Never married."

"Don't—" Malcolm shot out of his chair. "Matthew, what made you think hitting your brother with a coffee mug would be acceptable?"

Malcolm rushed across the room as John met him at the table, trusty towel in hand to mop up the spilled hot chocolate.

I watched as Malcolm wrapped his hand around Matthew's arm and leaned in to have a quiet—although intense looking—conversation. Matthew's lips tightened into a little pucker as his gaze shot toward me.

John straightened, watching the byplay between father and son before glancing my way.

When the quiet conversation ended, Malcolm straightened, gave the whole table a stern look, and headed back to me.

"Sorry about that."

"Um, no problem."

"So, we were talking about you. You've never been married. You work at a museum. How do you like that?"

"A lot actually. I'm lucky to do something I love. I handle the special events at a small private museum. Very select loan and viewing programs. My job lets me handle the events start to finish. It's always exciting to get to bring an idea from start to showing."

"That's…um, interesting. So, you do things like hang stuff on the walls?"

"Well, there's more to it than that. Hanging art is an art form in itself. If they aren't set up to be viewed properly, it can make or break the show. And not doing my job makes an artist look bad."

Malcolm just looked at me like that wasn't just a new idea, but a really boring, unimportant one.

"Your profile said you worked at Carmel Financial. What do you do there?"

"I'm a corporate advisor."

"I'm not sure I know what that means." I smiled at him, giving him the open to tell me about his job or change the topic.

"Really?"

I tried not to be insulted at the way he said it. As if I as stupid for not knowing what his job did.

"I assume you work with companies to do something financial."

"There's more to it than that." Malcolm launched into what would have been an excellent training video for new corporate advisors, but horrible for anyone who couldn't have cared less about corporations, advisors, or finances.

I'd started my 401k right away and hired a good planner because I wanted to retire one day. That was as smart as I was going to get about finances. Budget tightly and hire a good planner.

I know my weaknesses. I wasn't going to let them cost me my retirement.

But I also wasn't interested in what a planner—any planner—did every day, especially with corporations.

The only thing that broke up the lecture was his constant need to stop his kids from stealing each other's stuff, hurting one another, or destroying The Brew.

I was trying not to glaze over when a little body threw itself at Malcolm.

"Daddy, we've been here forever. You said she would be fun, but all she's done is sit there and drink her drink. I have to pee and Jeffery and Matthew said I have to go by myself, but I don't want to go in there alone. I don't know what's in there and my hot chocolate is cold and Matthew scribbled on my pony picture and I'm bored and you said we'd get ice cream after this."

"All right, you've been really good. Go tell your brothers to pack up."

I shuddered. If this was *good*, I was afraid to see what the little terrors were like if set on destruction.

"Sarah, would you mind?"

I glanced around trying to figure out what he was asking. "Would I mind?"

"Would you mind taking Amy to the ladies room?"

I stared at him waiting for the *just joking* that never came.

"Actually, yes I would mind. I don't know your daughter and I've never brought a little girl to the bathroom before. I'm afraid I'm not comfortable with that."

Malcolm set his hands on his hips as he stood over me—also probably waiting for the *just joking*.

"Really?"

"Yes. Really." How could this date not be over yet?

"Sarah, I thought we might have been a good match, but if you can't even do this one little thing, I'm not sure you're mother material."

"I never claimed to be mother material. But then again, you never claimed to be a father. So, I guess we're even."

I stayed seated, waiting for him to make his move. Waiting for him to take the terrors and head out.

He hovered, just watching and waiting. Waiting for what? Who knows?

Finally, he shook his head. "I'm not going to lie. I'm a little disappointed in you."

Really? I'm not the one who lied by omission all over my profile.

"Malcolm, I'm going to be honest here. You don't need a wife. You need a taskmaster of a nanny. I know that's a little more expensive, but it will save you money in the eLove membership fees."

I thought he was going to follow family suit and throw a hot beverage at me.

"Come on, kids. We're outta here."

And thank goodness.

The door was barely closed before John was filling the chair next to me.

"I can't believe how long you lasted." He sipped the tea he'd brought over with him. "I was ready to ask them to leave after the third hot chocolate spill."

"I'm so sorry."

"What are you sorry about?"

"I brought them here."

"Yeah, it totally sounded like you knew you were getting four-for-one when you showed up." John crossed his legs, one ankle over knee. "So, Date Three was shopping for a mommy, huh?"

"Looks that way. His kids aren't the best advertisement for the position."

"His kids are an advertisement for sterilization."

"John!"

"What? They're the worst behaved children I've had in here since I opened. And he was completely intrusive as a parent. Expecting others to entertain, admonish, and care for his children."

"I take it you're not a kid person."

"I love kids. Six nephews, three nieces. But if they ever threw a drink anywhere, let alone in public, they'd be standing up to eat for a few days not getting a new one." I watched his foot shake as he talked about his family, a whole new energy rushing through him. "They're smart and sweet. But just like all of us at that age, they have a little of the devil in them. It's our job as the adults in their lives to teach them what's not appropriate. And to teach it kindly with firmness."

Wow. I hadn't put a lot of thought into it, but that sounded like a pretty good plan to me.

"What about you? Kid person?"

Was I? I didn't have any siblings, so no nieces or nephews. All my friends with kids had newborns. I was pretty sure I wasn't a baby person. They were just starting to get personalities no matter what their parents said about a certain smile or the way they cooed.

39

Malcolm's kids definitely scared me a bit.

"I don't know." That was the most honest answer I had. "I haven't been around a lot of kids."

"You've got plenty of time to figure it out. And keep in mind they're not all like the terrors."

"Thanks, John." I finished my tea and set the mug on the tray. "I'm off. I have to realign some lights that burnt out at work."

"Sounds exciting. See you for Date Four."

I waved over my shoulder at his laugh and wondered if maybe I should have put him in charge of going through the profiles. Having a sober bartender on my team should be good for something.

SEVEN

Funny Guy looking for Fun Girl for casual dating – Yes, we all want more in our lives, but let's start slow and see where things lead.

I'D LEARNED MY LESSONS WITH Dates One through Three. I asked straight out about kids. I also felt around about guy friends and dating rules. Date Four said he had no kids, wanted to keep it that way for a while, and his guys always had his back.

Also, none of his other friends were on eLove. Yes. I asked.

We'd been emailing for two weeks and I was glad when he asked about meeting up. I was on the verge of pushing us to the face-to-face, but had been trying to leave that up to my top five.

Date Four, Hank, was a little different from One through Three. He was looking for someone to go out with, someone who wanted to hear some bands and see some movies. There wasn't any talk about the future. No *is this good for long-term* more *let's just wait and see*. It felt more like when you're meeting someone organically.

You don't bump into some cute guy at a party and say, "Oh, hi. Are you looking to get married in the next three-to-seven years?" If you did, that's probably something you should seek help for.

I'd considered inviting Four—I mean Hank—to a different spot to meet. Four fails in a row might be a little embarrassing. But John had been so encouraging that it didn't seem fair to deprive him of my possible humiliation.

When I got to The Brew, John was training a mostly-blond girl behind the counter. He pointed out different coffee and tea blends, showing her how to measure out the right amount for each serving size. After a moment, he introduced us like he was entertaining in his living room instead of running a business.

"Abby, this is Sarah. She's our dater."

Great. Just what I needed to be known for.

"So, you just come in here every day with different a date?"

It sounded more ridiculous when spoken aloud.

Especially when it was being spoken with disdain by someone who couldn't be over sixteen, had two piercings in her eyebrow, and whose hair was actually three shades not seen in nature under the blond bits.

"Not *every* day."

"Abby is my new employee." The pride John said it with was almost as obvious as when Jane introduced Dahlia to people.

"Nice to meet you." I wasn't sure it really was. I hadn't been this nervous around a teenage girl since I was a teenage girl.

"Is that what you're wearing?"

Since I was obviously wearing what I was wearing, I wasn't sure how to answer that question. "Yes?"

"And this is a first date?"

"A casual one."

Abby quirked that pierced eyebrow and moved away.

"So, Date Four tonight, huh?" John set out a tray and began mixing a new blend for me. "Who's this one?"

"A marketing executive looking to date casually."

"Oh. Casually." He might as well have said, *Oh. To slaughter kittens.*

"What?"

"Nothing."

"No. What was that all about?"

John ignored me and headed around the counter to set my tea tray on my usual table.

"John."

"I just didn't think you were the *casual* type of girl." Yes. He did put air quotes around it. And he sounded really annoyed. As if I'd put out an ad for sex.

"What is that supposed to mean?"

"Come on, Sarah. Casual is obviously code for sex. Casual sex."

"No it isn't." Was it? *Had* I accidentally put out an ad for sex?

"Of course it is. He said he's just looking for someone to have fun with?"

"So?"

"So, fun is also code for sex."

"Not everything is code for sex." I was really hoping not everything was code for sex. "I mean, if I asked you for more hot water, that doesn't have anything to do with sex."

"I bet Scarlett Johansson could make that about sex. You actually used the word hot. We're halfway there."

I just shook my head at him. I wasn't going to let John derail Date Four before the poor guy even got here.

"I'll be right over there." John pointed to the counter, as if he'd magically become my body guard, or in case I thought he might be somewhere else—like shopping in New York or something.

I settled into the chair, picking up the coffee table book that had appeared in the last few days. It was a photo documentary of coffee bean farms in South America. The colors were remarkable, along with the gorgeous landscapes. It was easy to lose myself in the pages.

Finally, Date Four showed up about fifteen minutes late, looking like he'd been chased by the paparazzi. Disheveled, dark glasses...all he needed was a trench coat.

"Sarah? Sorry I'm late. Parking was crazy." It never dawned on me someone would drive the two miles instead of jumping on the train.

"No problem. You must be Hank. It's great to meet you." I folded the coffee table book up and slid it back onto the table. "Do you want to grab something to drink?"

"That's okay." He settled into the chair next to me.

I couldn't help but be a little annoyed. I knew he was late, but John was trying to run a business here. Instead, Hank angled the chair toward me, shifting it so the arms were touching.

"So, Sarah, did you have a good weekend? What did you do?"

The soft step-in was different. Usually guys asked more about work or something on my profile or if I was enjoying eLove. Not something as normal as what I did that weekend.

It immediately put me at ease. John was wrong. This wasn't all about sex. This guy was actually trying to get to know me, not just my shiny profile.

"I went out and saw my best friend. She moved to the suburbs, so it's a bit of a trip. And I saw the new Bond movie. Always a treat."

Look at me nonchalantly tossing out my action movie preference. The dating books had said to shy away from mentioning chick flicks or anything too girly. Granted, a few hours staring at one of the hottest men on the silver screen wasn't exactly non-girly...but I loved when they blew stuff up too.

"Did you like it? I wasn't sure I was going to with how they're stepping further away from the classics."

"It was great. Just enough of the old-school polish to *feel* like a Bond movie, but enough updates to keep it interesting."

Hank dove into a conversation about his favorite James Bonds over the years. He knew Sean Connery wasn't the first and argued Moore wasn't the worst. It was great to just relax and chat about something more comfortable than where I saw myself in five years.

I was beginning to think casual was the right way to start things—to not be looking for Mr. Serious Right Now. All the other dates felt like interviews next to this.

"I have to say, you're much prettier than I expected."

"Really?" I thought I looked exactly like the three pictures I'd picked out. Jane tried to get me to post one from her wedding, but I'd been professionally done up for the event. It felt like false advertising.

"I've found women—*normal* women—are pretty honest in their profiles."

"How do you define not normal?"

"I'm not really into high maintenance girls."

"So, I'm not high maintenance. That's usually a plus."

"For me it is." He sat back and stretched out, his arms spanning across the back of the chair next to his. "I know some guys like all the drama of a high maintenance woman and the type of relationship that brings. But personally, I just want someone I can be myself with."

"I know—"

It might have been how empty The Brew was. Or it might have been how the door slammed against the wall really hard, but my attention jerked to the woman silhouetted in its frame.

"Oh, hell no." The strained, shrill voice filled the room as the woman marched toward us.

Next to me, Hank leapt to his feet and turned to face her as she barreled through the café, pushing chairs out of her way instead of weaving around them.

"Who the hell is this?" She jabbed a finger my direction.

I was beginning to get the idea I was in the middle of a very heated, very old war.

This wasn't looking like the best place to be standing right now.

"I'm Sarah." I offered my hand, trying to smooth out whatever was going on.

"Sarah? Sarah Home-Wrecker? Is that your full name? Then you just go standing there smiling at me and think I'll shake your hand? You think that's how it works?"

She started to make her way around my chair, but I shifted to keep it between us—a barrier of wood-framed cotton.

"I'm sorry. I'm not really sure what's going on here."

But I was afraid I had a decent idea.

"Adultery. That's what. You think you can just date another woman's husband and it's okay?"

"Absolutely not. I just met him online. This is our first get-together. He told me he was single."

"Sure he did."

I glanced at Hank as I edged away from both of them, trying to get around the oversized coffee table. John was gone, but his new teen was leaning against the counter, her chin propped on both hands.

"I swear. I did *not* know he was married. I'm looking for a guy of my own. I wouldn't share one and I definitely wouldn't steal one."

Hank still stood there, off to the side, looking like a deer who knew what was coming behind the headlights.

"Tell her." I picked up my napkin and threw it at him to get his attention. "Tell her you lied to me and we just met today."

"I didn't really *lie* to you."

What? What was wrong with these people?

"I very clearly remember asking if you were single."

"No." Hank crossed his arms, giving me a look that said he thought this was my fault. "You asked me if I was *dating* anyone."

I was going to kill him myself.

"Okay, let me clarify. When a woman asks you if you're dating—or seeing—someone, she's asking if you're single." I picked up the spoon that had been sitting on the napkin I'd just thrown at him. Then I threw the spoon at him too. "Here's a clue Einstein—married is not single."

Just as my voice started to rise, the woman jumped over the table and grabbed my arm.

"Don't you throw things at him. You don't get to throw things at him." She shook me and, as her free hand came up, I snapped out of it just in time to dodge her slap.

Both my arms came up to block my face, taking the blow across my wrists. And then a second one.

"Hey! I'm not the one cheating on you! I don't even know you."

I blocked another swing.

"Ruth!"

You'd think it would be Hank who stepped in to get her under control. You'd be wrong. Another woman pounded through the doorway, her walk brisk, her attention focused.

The third blow never came as the woman, Ruth, turned toward the voice.

"Sounds like this isn't the girl's fault." The second woman stopped next to Ruth, looking me over. "Not worth your time. Neither is this worthless boy who can't manage to stay faithful for more than a week at a go."

"Drea," Hank finally spoke up. Glaring down at the new woman, he took a step toward her. "I told you to stay out of our marriage. Your sister doesn't need you barging in all the time and shaking the hornet's nest."

"I'm not shaking anything. You're a cheating S.O.B. She needs to get as far away from you as possible."

"Drea, please." Ruth's voice had softened, almost to a pleading level. "Don't upset him. I just want things to go back the way they were."

"When, Ruth? When do you want them to go back to? He's been cheating on you since you met him. There're no good times to go back to. There's only the time before you knew. Is that what you want? You want to just not know? If that's it, then you need to quit following him and checking his email and his phone. If you just want to not know, stop looking. But if you think there's a time to go back to when he was completely faithful, then you're deluded."

I stepped back again, hoping to fade into the background, but afraid to draw attention to myself if I tried to walk away.

Plus, walking away would mean turning my back on the crazy people.

Speaking of which—I glanced toward the counter. Abby-the-Trainee still stood there enraptured by the drama unrolling in front of her. All she needed was popcorn. And yet, still no John.

"Drea." Hank was finally getting involved in this train wreck, stepping over the coffee table to come between the two women. "What goes on between me and Ruth is between us. I don't recall you taking vows at our wedding."

"No. This is what goes on between you and Ruth and..." Drea waved a hand in my direction, "every slutty girl you meet as soon as you leave the house."

"Hey now." I was so insulted I forgot I was trying to stay out of it. "Some of us aren't slutty. We're lied to. And now, we're leaving."

Ruth made a grab at my arm again, but her sister stopped her.

"It's not her fault. You need to put the blame in the right place."

I thought for a second Ruth was going to wind up and take a swing at Drea. Instead, after a long moment, one tear slipped down her cheek.

"I know, but I don't know what I'll do."

"You'll come stay with me. We'll get you a good attorney."

"Wait just a second." Hank tried to get around the table again, but Drea was pushing Ruth toward the front door. "Ruth is my wife. She's not going anywhere but home with me."

Ruth turned, her anger finally focused in the right place.

"I'm not going anywhere with you. I'm tired of this. I'm tired of being lied to." She picked up my tea cup and threw it at him. "And humored." This time it was the creamer. "And cheated on."

You'd think with all the small stuff gone, she'd be out of weapons. But Ruth was obviously an aggressive woman. She picked up the now empty tea tray and swung at Hank's head like he was a fastball coming at her in the seventh inning.

The first swing made a solid connection with his shoulder.

"Hey!" Hank ducked away, trying to outpace his enraged wife.

The next swing caught him across the back of the head.

"Ruth, stop it."

But she kept swinging, chasing him around the coffee shop while he tried to stay out of her way. After a minute, she had him cornered, the tray raised over her head, when a voice came from behind us.

"Put the tea tray down and back away. I won't put up with any more of this nonsense in my shop."

I half turned, still afraid to give the crazy people my back, to find John standing there, balancing on the balls of his feet like he was ready pounce.

Everyone froze—Hank with his hands blocking his head, Ruth with the tray over hers, and Drea looking smug.

"That is more than enough. I don't go into your home and tear it up. If you have a personal issue with one another, this is not the place." John strode across the café, picking up the broken pieces of porcelain as he went, and wrenched the tray out Ruth's hands. "That's going to be five dollars for the cup, twelve for the creamer, and twenty-five for the wrecked tea tray. Whose card do you want to put that on?"

EIGHT

DATING TRUTH #4: There's always another fish in the sea...it's just that we keep dumping toxic waste in the water so who knows what you'll catch next.

I STOOD WHERE I WAS, too scared to move as John rang Hank up, charging him for all the broken items and my tea. The two women waited at the door, identical expressions of rage on their faces.

The irrational part of me was annoyed yet another date had been a failure. The irrational part also wanted an apology for the assault.

The rational side just wanted them out of there as quickly as possible.

Once they left, John scanned the room, his gaze hard.

"You." He pointed at me. "Sit over there and don't move."

I headed toward the far side of the room where he'd assigned me and collapsed into a chair, just glad to have something under me.

"You." He pointed at the teen audience member who had enjoyed every second of my torture. "Clean that up and then you and I are going to talk."

Abby grumbled as she grabbed a broom and dustpan. I slumped over the table, setting my head on my crossed arms and hoping John would go have that word with Abby first.

Instead, a light touch brushed my shoulder, pushing my hair to the side and letting the light into my little self-made cave.

"Are you okay?"

"Yes." I mumbled, barely able to hear myself.

"Sarah, look at me." He squatted next to me leaving no option but for me to meet his gaze. "Are. You. Okay?"

I nodded, realizing I was more embarrassed than anything—and guilty. I felt so guilty about John's lovely coffee shop getting torn up like that.

"John, I'm so sorry about all the craziness. I had no idea."

"Of course you didn't. You're not the type of girl who goes out with married men."

Well, at least *someone* realized that.

"And your poor tea tray. I can't believe she broke your stuff."

"Don't worry about that. I bought everything in bulk. I have at least two boxes of stuff in the basement I haven't even opened."

"But you charged them for it…"

"Of course I did. I wasn't going to let them off the hook. You can't reinforce crazy behavior with dismissive attitudes."

That made sense, in a weird John kind of way.

"I think maybe I'll start doing my meet-ups somewhere else."

Because I didn't like the idea of putting John out like this again. And also because I couldn't stand the thought of him seeing me in yet another humiliating situation. He was seeing me at my lowest, over and over again, and then once more.

"Absolutely not. You'll meet the rest of those guys here. I don't want you out of my sight until we know you're not meeting up with some crazy person. This could have been far worse. That guy was just a jerk and his wife was just ticked off. What if they really were nuts?" He stood and shook his head. "No. You'll meet them here."

I could all but hear the *Where I can keep an eye on you* he didn't say. I'd never had a big brother, but I suspect they eyed you like that quite often.

"All right. But any structural damage done is strictly your fault. You've been warned."

I waited for him to change his mind, to take the out. Instead, he grinned. "I think I can handle it. Now, why don't you head home before you incite a full-on riot?"

He was giving me far more credit than I deserved.

NINE

DATING TRUTH #5: The best way to put a bad date behind you is doing something you love...unless the something you love is just more dating. Don't do that.

THE HOLIDAY SEASON WAS COMING to a head—only two days until Christmas. Everyone was rushing around with shopping bags of gifts to wrap and food to cook. I had one gift I was really looking forward to giving, and it meant going to the coffee shop.

I got to The Brew an hour early, a box securely tucked under my arm.

Once again, John was nowhere to be seen. But Abby -- lucky me – was front and center at the counter looking like she'd remembered to bring popcorn for today's potential fiasco.

"Is John here?"

"Yes."

"Can I talk to him?"

"No."

I really hoped he was working on her counter-side manner.

"Why not?"

"He's on the phone with someone he keeps calling sweetheart."

Sweetheart? Interesting.

"Why didn't you just say he was on the phone?"

"You didn't ask."

I wasn't even going to argue the point. I was already learning when it came to Abby to just stay as far away from actual conversation as possible.

"Can you bring me a ladder?"

Luckily, Abby was more interested in what kind of mischief I was up to than creating trouble.

I unpacked the box, pulled out my toolbox, folder, and the hardware I'd bought and set it up on a table where I could reach everything easily.

Abby came back, toting an eight-step. Perfect. She eyed the table with its tools and then glared hard at me.

"I'm not sure I should let you do whatever you're about to do."

"And yet you let a woman hit me. More than once. Shocking." I unfolded the ladder and pushed the step locks into place. "Don't get in the way. This is my Christmas present to John. If he's on the phone, then it could be a surprise. So just...do what you do. Over there."

I pointed back toward the counter, too tired and too anxious about Date Five to be more polite.

Plus, polite had gone out the window when she'd watched my assault as if it were the latest *Housewives* show.

"Sarah?"

"Yes?" I glanced down from where I was measuring the lights on the ceiling.

"John told me I have to tell you I'm sorry for not helping you out or getting him or calling the cops or something the other day."

As apologies went, that one was pretty much a failure.

"Are you?" I shouldn't have asked. I should have just said okay and went back to work.

Abby looked at her feet, one finger twirling a pink-tipped lock.

"I'm sorry if you got hurt."

Well, that was a little better. The girl was painfully honest. Not to mention tactless and unkind. The exact opposite of John. How long could this mentorship last? And did her honesty extend to her own actions? I could only hope so. Because if she wasn't, John's soft heartedness could come back and really bite him in the rear.

"So, what are you doing with the lights?"

I was about to say, *changing them,* before I looked down and saw she was actually paying attention.

"I bought lighting fixtures that will allow him to showcase the art better. He had the wrong fixtures and the wrong bulbs. The wattage was way off. A large part of what sells art is how it's displayed."

"Because people are so superficial." She stated it. It wasn't a question.

I took in a deep breath and prayed for patience. Abby had been rubbing me wrong since the beginning and I couldn't figure out if it was that or the surety of her attitude that annoyed me.

"No. Because art that isn't lit well, doesn't show well. It would be like picking out music on an old cell phone. You wouldn't know what it really sounds like. Here," I motioned at the wall. "People don't know what the art really looks like. The lighting will help them see it. It will also look more professional without creating a spot-like focus or an overly bright area and ruin the feel of the room."

I took one of the paintings off the wall to see how they were hung, checked the fixtures, and climbed back down.

"But first, I need to lower all the paintings. They're hung too high. It's like dating a guy you always have to look waaayyyy up at. You get a crick in your neck no matter how hot he is."

I could have sworn she almost smiled.

"If you want to help, you can take the paintings down and lean them against the wall. I'll start moving the set-ups."

I tried not to show my surprise when she did.

With Abby's help, I moved all the paintings, switched out the four lights, and hung the new matte cream placards I'd made next to each piece.

We were already cleaning up when John came out of the backroom, mid-sentence through his next thing for Abby. "What are you guys doing?"

"Merry Christmas!" I was so excited I jumped off the last two rungs of the ladder and rushed over to pull him forward. "I relit your wall. You now have a museum quality wall with placards. Check it out." I pointed to the fresh new descriptions hanging beside each painting.

"Wow." He stared—just stared at the wall.

It dawned on me he may not have liked someone coming in and changing his shop around, even if they were paid a lot to do it professionally.

"Um, it's okay, right? That I changed it?"

"I helped." Abby stood next to the ladder with a weird expression, halfway between hopeful and defiant, bringing her lips together in what looked like it was trying to be a grin.

She hadn't waited. She'd stepped up to take the heat with me, or the thank you, but she hadn't left me out there on my own.

That apology—the really lame one she'd given me twenty minutes before – I mentally accepted it right then.

"No. This is great. I just...I just didn't expect it." John walked past me to stand a few feet from the wall. "It really does make a difference, doesn't it?"

I stood back, enjoying my work.

"This is great. Thank you." He turned, looking down at me with that soft smile of his.

It must have been the light because I hadn't realized how dark his eyes were, or that he had a bunch of freckles over the bridge of his nose, or how tall he was. Okay, so I'd noticed he wasn't my type of tall, but I guess five-ten was taller than I gave it credit for. Poor five-ten.

Plus, my world was filled with hard-polished guys. They just typically felt...bigger, larger than life.

"Not a problem. You've been great about the mess of dates I've had here. I figured it was the least I could do. Maybe you'll get more artists coming in if they see how strong your wall looks now."

"This is, truly, the nicest gift."

"I really just wanted to do something nice for you...a *thank you.*"

"Best thank you ever. But, Sarah, you don't have to thank me."

Awww...

"What are friends for? And cafes? If you can't have crazy first dates in a café, where can you have them?"

This was true.

But they were so much easier when you shared them with a friend.

TEN

DATING TRUTH #6: When you can't get any lower, there's always a smug girl with a boyfriend there to knock the emotional step out from under you.

I 'M LOOKING FORWARD TO MEETING this guy of yours." Claire had barely let me get my coat off before she started.

"How about you ladies? I'm looking forward to meeting all your guys too." Deflect! Deflect!

All the girls shifted to look my way. I half hoped one of them would come to my rescue. But Claire was driving this boat and no one was going to get in the way. I'd already talked to Becca anyway. She'd called me Christmas Eve to wish me happy holidays

I was counting on Angie to have great news.

Or not.

"Yes," Claire drawled. "But you never talk about your mystery man."

"I'm...I don't know. You know when something feels too good to be true? It just comes out of nowhere and bam!—hits you over the head? I keep waiting to find out I was making it all up in my overactive imagination."

Claire mumbled something that sounded suspiciously like 'me too' before she was interrupted by the waiter.

"Why don't you guys tell me about your dates?" If I couldn't divert Claire, I could at least get the others chatting. Plus, I was actually interested in how things were going for Becca and Angie.

Becca launched into a description of the perfect holiday weekend. Airplane Guy had gone to visit her on the twenty-sixth and then flown the New York leg again. Everything was joy and happiness and mistletoe.

Angie was disappointed Jonathan wasn't able to spend Christmas with them, but she convinced her brother they weren't just sleeping together. That they were both serious. A call from Jonathan solidified that, and there was joy and happiness and unused mistletoe in the Brockman house.

Claire spent Christmas with her family and Marcus. I can only assume she found her version of joy and happiness shopping while he worked. I didn't want to know about the mistletoe.

As we wrapped up the meal, I handed Claire a check for the additional seat at our New Year's Eve table. Part of me hated to do it, but I knew if I waited till that night it would be even worse.

"Oh, honey. Why don't you keep your money until we see if you need the seat?"

"I need the seat." I said it as nicely as possible, pretending I didn't know what she was really saying. Also pretending that she wasn't right. "Plus, it's not like we can cancel a seat at this point anyway."

As soon as I said it, she got that look. That my-life-is-so-great-I-feel-bad-for-you look.

"Right. So, I'll see you on New Year's."

With Mr. Right. As soon as I found him.

ELEVEN

Love Again – I'm a widower who is looking to start the next part of my life. I know what a blessing a good relationship can be and want to share that knowledge and feeling with the right woman.

I WAS A LITTLE NERVOUS about Date Five. So many worries. Could I—if we got serious—deal with being with someone who had loved another woman that much?

There was such a difference between losing someone and leaving someone. I just wasn't sure.

But Date Five, otherwise known as Dave, sounded like a great guy. We'd been emailing since the first week and had moved to talking on the phone the second. He'd sent me a lovely little email while he'd been out of town for Christmas.

Now, December twenty-eighth, I was beginning to wonder if I'd ever find anyone, let alone a date for New Year's Eve.

I swung into The Brew feeling as if I'd come home for the holidays myself. I hadn't seen John—or Abby for that matter—since I'd given John his Christmas gift. After the day trip down to see my mom at her condo with her current husband—number five—where I sat through a meal where she counted my calories for me—six-hundred-and-twenty—and played with her collection of cats—three—I basically counted the hours till I could head home again.

Needless to say, my mother wasn't the highlight of my season.

Three days later I was still trying to recover from hearing about everyone who was married, how my career was boring, and how size eight was the new size twelve so maybe I should drop some weight.

I considered dropping one hundred and forty pounds in the form of my mother.

But The Brew? It was peaceful and easy. It was a comfy escape where I could chill out and be myself. It was—

"You look like you gained five pounds in your face over Christmas. What exactly did you eat?" Abby stood behind the counter, eyeing me as if I was trying to slip something past her.

"I'm sorry. Mom, is that you?"

"Whatever." She turned around and started putting my tea tray together while I stripped my coat and mittens off and hung them over a chair by the fire.

Glancing around, I was surprised to take in three filled tables. This was exactly the holiday cheer John needed for his business.

"Where's John?"

"Do I look like his keeper?"

"Kind of. You definitely like to keep track of everyone's business."

"Fine. He's out back doing something on his computer."

Huh. Probably some Numbers Guy finance stuff to reboot his new year.

I paid for my tea and carried the tray to my regular chair. On the coffee table was a little sign that said *Reserved at 3pm*. How sweet.

I checked out the art wall and saw someone had added a sign-up sheet for the artist's mailing list. I wished I'd thought of that myself. There were even two names on it that weren't John, Sarah, or Abby, so huge win.

Five of three, I settled into my chair to wait. If I'd learned anything over the last four weeks, it was patience was key in the process. You waited to see if anyone contacted you. If you Whistled or Messaged first, you waited to hear back. You waited to hear back again once you returned their message. Then you waited more. Then you waited to see if they'd want to talk. Then you waited to see if they wanted to get together. Even if you were the person suggesting it, you waited for an answer. Then you waited for them to show up.

I'd probably waited twenty hours this month.

That was roughly the amount of time a new exhibit took me to set up.

Food for thought.

At five past, I started to wonder. No one but Married Guy Hank had been late, and Dave just didn't strike me as the rude or thoughtless type.

At ten past, John wandered out and perched on the arm of the chair next to me.

"So, Date Five. Your final Crayon."

Some things you never live down.

I glanced at my phone to check the time and saw my email alert. I knew it was bad news as soon as I saw Dave's email address.

Sarah,

I'm so sorry to back out on you at the last minute. I realized as I was about to leave I'm just not ready to start dating. I've really enjoyed our chats and I'm sure if I'd shown up I would have left hoping we could be friends. I know that wasn't the point. So, I'll wish you luck and know whoever snaps you up is a luckier man than I.

Best,

Dave

What does it say that one of the sweetest things a guy had said to me in years was a brush off letter?

"It can't be that bad?" John slid into the chair and started to lean in to look at the email before stopping himself. "No one's puppy died, right?"

"No. No puppy. Just my hope for the future."

"Your guy *died?*" Now he leaned in and snatched the phone. "Who even knew to email you?"

"He didn't die." I fought an eye roll and then gave in. He deserved it. "He canceled."

John read the email and grimaced. "I need a copy of this. If I ever dump a girl without actually going out with her, this is perfect."

"Are you saying I'm not great?"

"Um. No. Of course not. You're awesome. Really awesome."

"Yeah. Uh-huh."

"Don't let the Dates bring you down." I thought he was going to wave a fist in the air.

"Maybe I should try one last time. Or just ask Jane to set me up with someone for the night. Just be straight with the guy and admit I need a boyfriend for the night. But it feels horrible and stupid to have a fake date." I sighed as I reread Dave's email. "I'd feel like such a loser."

John handed me my phone and leaned back, settling in for what was probably going to be a long lecture.

"Do you really need a guy to enjoy your night? Does it matter that much? We just established you're awesome."

"I am *totally* awesome."

"So, why do you need a guy for this? What do you really need to prove to those girls?"

"Well, I'd been telling them I was seeing someone since November. I've kind of painted myself into a corner."

John watched me, that yeah-so-what look on his face.

"I know. It's my own fault." I said before he could agree with me. "I was being prideful and look where it got me. But I panicked. You don't know what it's like."

My voice had risen, causing people on the other side of the room to look our way.

"What what's like?"

"To be her. *That* girl. The last single girl. Your close friends are paired off. Your not so close friends are paired off. Your acquaintances are paired off. The people you know casually who you don't even like are paired off. And everyone just looks at you like...Like you're a failure and a loser. Mothers lecture. Aunts lecture. Women you barely know say things like *Bless your heart* or *There's someone out there for everyone, even you*. Seriously? I can't be her. I can't be the last single girl."

"Sarah, after hearing about these girls, I can tell you one sounds nice, one seems okay, and one sounds like a man's worst nightmare. Now, next to a really awesome person, none of those girls look very good."

I smiled, trying not to cry at his kind words or my sick feeling of defeat. I wrapped my hand around his where it rested on the chair's arm. "John, you're seriously one of the best people I know. Now, I'm going home to panic." I gave his hand a squeeze and stood. "Thanks for everything."

"You're going to stop by on your way, right? Abby and I want to see you all dressed up." He rose and walked me out. "Maybe get some pictures. Just like prom, only with twenties garb and drinking."

"And no date."

John just shook his head at me. "You're a mess. A really nice mess, but still."

I headed out, slightly relieved for the dating part to be over. I was done with the crazies. The only one allowed to drive me nuts was my own subconscious. She was doing a good enough job for everyone.

TWELVE

DATING TRUTH #7: Wine. Lots of Wine.

W E'RE BACK HERE!"

I made my way back to the creamy yellow kitchen where Jane stirred away at something on the stove while Dahlia played on a bright matt near the glass door.

"It's just us tonight. Matt went to watch the game with his guys."

"You mean you threw him out so we could have girl's night in."

"Yes. That's what marriage is all about. Knowing when to throw your spouse out and the spouse knowing to leave."

I'm pretty sure she was kidding.

"Here." She handed me a bottle of white wine. "Open that puppy up. It's perfect for the salmon. And while you do, I want a rundown of the online dating mission."

"Don't you want to know about my holidays? Or tell me about whatever run-in you had with your mother-in-law? Or about what people bought Dahlia for Christmas?"

"Nope. None of the above. Online dating for two-thousand, Alec."

I'd known it was going to come down to that, but I thought we'd ease into it. At least let me drink a little wine first.

But once Jane got an idea in her head, there was no getting it out, so over a glass of wine—okay, two—I gave her a summary of each date. In retrospect, they were funny. From the near perfect to the near homicidal, I'd had quite a run.

"Tell me more about this John guy."

"John? What about him?"

"I don't know. How old is he? How tall is he? Does he have all his hair?"

"Wow, Jane. Superficial much?" I loved her like a sister, but the getting-on-John-about-his-looks thing wasn't cool.

"No. Not superficial. But it's the only thing I don't know about him and I feel like I must be missing something."

"What do you mean?"

She looked at me like I might be a moron, then shook her head as if she'd finally decided I was.

"All night it's been John this and John that. John makes me this tea. John threw the guy out. John loved my Christmas present...which by the way, where the heck is *my* Christmas gift? This John guy got something and I didn't? And he sounds nice and funny and smart. He's successful and well off and gave up a high power career to do something he loves. He's close to his family and spoils his nephews and nieces? Am I forgetting anything?"

Well, no. And when she put it like that, he sounded pretty darn great.

"Right," Jane went on. "So, he must be old or fat or ugly or smelly or short or something really unattractive. What's wrong with him?"

"Well..." I racked my brain trying to give her an answer she'd accept. "He just got out of a relationship a few months ago."

"You told me about that. The stupid ex-girlfriend who was looking to be part of a power couple." Jane waved her hand as if I'd brought up something insignificant. "What else could it be? You're just not attracted to him?"

"I...That is, John is..." I tried to put words around it, around John, but all I could come up with were positives. "He's thirty or thirty-one. About three inches taller than me. He has all this hair. It just does whatever it wants. I'm betting his admin was in charge of reminding him to cut it. He runs his hands through it and it just stands on end. Of course he doesn't smell funny. He smells like lemon. Probably because of work. There's nothing *wrong* with him. It's just..."

"What?"

"He's John." As soon as the words left my mouth I panicked. "Oh my gosh. He's John."

All the hairs on my arm stood up as heat rushed over my skin. Jane must have seen the panic because she poured me a third glass of wine.

"Jane. How could you do this to me?"

"Sarah..."

"Don't *Sarah* me. How am I going to face him? Everything was fine until you pointed this out. What if I'm falling in love with him?" I sucked in a breath. "Oh no. I think he's dating someone."

"What? How can he be dating someone? You never mentioned that."

"It didn't matter thirty seconds ago!"

Did she not understand what she'd done?

"Okay. Back up. What makes you think he's dating someone?"

"When I asked him about online dating, he said he'd rather try the old-fashioned way first. And, lately he's been out back on the phone or his laptop whenever I come in. Just in the last few weeks."

"That doesn't mean he's dating someone."

"He also made a crack about needing Date Five's email brushing me off in case he ever didn't show up for a date."

"Still, that could have just been a joke."

"And he talks to someone on the phone he calls sweetheart. Who the heck is this sweetheart chick?" My voice jumped up another octave and Dahlia looked at me like I was a confusing new toy. "Plus, through all this, he's never asked me out. And he knows how desperate I am for someone to go to the New Year's thing with. That would have been a perfect chance. But he didn't suggest it. *And* he said he has to close early New Year's. He must already have plans."

"Oh. Well, that stinks."

"*Jane.*" What was I going to do? How was I going to go back in there and face him with all these swirly feelings? This was a disaster. And when she started coming in for all those dinners by the fire and working or reading while he closed up, how was I going to stick around for that? And Abby had only insulted me once this week. That was progress. I was going to lose it all. There was no way I was going to watch him get serious with someone.

"Come on. You said he wasn't your type. Too soft. And all that hair."

"I like his hair." Oh no. I like his hair. I was doomed. Doomed.

I pictured cool autumn nights, walking from the gym after work to the cozy chairs by the fire. Ordering in different meals. Or maybe occasionally trying to cook something and testing it out on him. Games and books and conversation and coffee. Bringing my work I'd do at home and tucking myself into a corner. All of it centered around John.

It sounded delightful.

I was more than doomed. I was whatever came after doomed.

I needed a romance time machine to get rid of this epiphany. Or maybe just more wine. I laid my head on my arms and tried to think of anything but John.

"Here." Jane opened a new bottle and filled my glass.

What were best friends for?

THIRTEEN

DATING TRUTH #8: When faced with the man of your dreams, the only thing to do is play it cool. Or at least play dumb.

I SUCKED IN A DEEP, cold breath before pushing my way into The Brew Ha Ha.

Everything would be fine. Everything would be the same. Nothing would be different. I would not act like a complete idiot.

Or, at least, that's what I'd been telling myself all the way over.

Inside, Abby and John were cleaning out the brewers, getting ready for their early close.

"Hey guys." I stood back, afraid to approach. I didn't want them to see how nervous I was. All it would take was one of Abby's comments and I was dead in the water.

"You're here." John climbed down off his step ladder to come around the counter. "Let's see your Roaring Twenties look."

Sadly, I'd put a lot of thought into this. When Claire had suggested the dinner months ago, I'd been excited to go just for the excuse to buy a flapper dress. And since I was going to crash and burn on every other level tonight, I went all out—the dress, the shoes, the beads. I'd even had my hair and make-up done. The stylist had tucked my hair so it looked like I'd gotten a bob.

I was looking pretty good if I did say so myself.

"Did you cut your hair?" He looked a bit shocked. Or maybe it just reminded him he hadn't had his cut in a few months.

"No, it's just the way it's done."

"Oh. Good. You look great. Are you carrying a flask in your garter?"

"A girl never tells these things." I gave him a wink, figuring if I just hammed it up I'd stop feeling like I was going to confess my newfound feelings any second.

"Did you decide to borrow a guy from your friend Jane?"

Even I was surprised at the laugh that rushed out of me. "Nope. I decided instead to deal with Claire and just get over her. And it."

"Good for you." John glanced toward Abby, probably to make sure no snide comments were coming my way. "So, tell me, where is this party?"

"It's in the ballroom at the historic house over on Lake."

"I've always wanted to see it. We had a corporate event there, but I was stuck at work." He shook his head, probably remembering, then glanced around the shop. "Man, I totally love my life now."

It took everything in me not to ask if it was because of his new girlfriend.

Back on topic.

"Getting to see the house is part of the reason I wanted to go. I hear they have an awesome private gallery. Maybe I can get a security guard drunk and flirt my way in."

"I'm sure you could do it. Or you could just give him your card and ask to see it. Probably less police involved that way."

"Oh, John. Always the voice of reason."

"It's true. A burden I have to carry throughout my days." He wiped his hands on the ever present towel and nodded his head toward the counter. "Want some tea? You're running a little early, aren't you?"

"I can't. I promised to stop by work after I was dressed. They're having a New Year's Eve event. We're renting the space out, so I don't have to work it, but they wanted me to just come in and make sure everything was going like it should."

"They're going to love your new look."

"I'm tempted to buy a few more. Maybe I can bring the beaded mini-dress back."

I stood there, grinning up at him like an idiot—noticing his hair and his dimple and the freckles on the bridge of his nose and the flecks of green surprising me in his brown eyes. Just noticing.

"So…" John's eyebrows lifted, probably in an unspoken *Why are you looking at me like that? Please stop and back away* quirk.

"Right. So, I should get to work. And then off to face the vultures."

"It's going to be fine." He sounded so sure.

"I wish I had your confidence."

"It's easy to be confident. I've watched you handle everything short of a natural disaster with all those dates. If you could get through those, then tonight is going to be a piece of cake."

When put like that, I almost believed him.

Now it was just a matter of embracing my singleness and telling Claire where she could put her cat claws.

FOURTEEN

DATING TRUTH #9: I am woman, hear me roar. That's right, do not tick me off.

WHILE MY CAB WAITED ITS turn, I watched the line ahead of me as one made-up person after another climbed out and handed over their keys or paid off the cabbie. It was going to be a long night. I'd thought about getting there late or, at the very least, right as things were starting. Leave as little room for all the smug Claire comments and group pity as possible.

But then I got annoyed. Annoyed at Claire. Annoyed at the other girls for not standing up to her. Annoyed at myself for caring, for not standing up for myself. Annoyed it mattered that I was it. That everyone else was ready to climb on Noah's ark and I was the last of my kind. Just like the poor unicorn.

The point of having friends was not just to have people to do stuff with, but to have people who had your back. Who were there for you.

I may have been the Last Single Girl, but I had been for longer than I realized. The Alphabet didn't count because I'd never let myself get close to Becca and Angie because of Claire.

Again. Claire.

And whose fault was that?

I paid the driver when we got to the door and headed in. Claire could say what she wanted, but I was out, I looked amazing, and it was New Year's Eve. If she wanted to try to ruin it for me, she was going to have to do something extreme. Like burn the building down, or show my junior high pictures on a Jumbotron.

I brushed through the entry, dropping my wrap off at the coatroom and scanning the party. It was mostly groups of friends, a few tables of women. True to its name, the booze was already flowing and the prohibition themed drinks were being passed around like people were liquoring up before a raid.

A large man at the door stopped me as I went to step into the crowd.

"Ticket?"

Leave it to Claire. It didn't dawn on me we'd have to have a ticket. I'd seen her four days ago. I'd *paid* her four days ago. I couldn't help but wonder if this was a power play, if she'd oops-forgotten-air-quotes my ticket.

Make that tickets. Plural.

"I'm with Claire Christel's group. She has the tickets. I'm Sarah Gable."

The man picked up a clipboard from the stand behind him and flipped through. "Gable. Sarah. I have you down here as two tickets."

He glanced behind me as if I was hiding a date.

Geez. I wasn't going to take it from a doorman too.

"It looks like I'm here solo, doesn't it? Not that there's anything wrong with that or it has anything to do with the unreliableness of your gender. Maybe, before you start doing that look-around-innocently mocking thing, you should stop and wonder exactly what he did to manage to not be here on New Year's Eve, right?"

"Um. Sorry Ms. Gable. You're at Table Eight."

The seventh wheel at table eight for eight. Of course I was.

I made a beeline for the bar, planning to pick up a drink, and if I was lucky a date.

I hadn't even made it through the line when the goosebumps raced down my spine. Definitely a Wicked Witch alert.

"Sarah, we're so glad you made it." Claire clung to a huge man. He was easily six-three and could probably bench lift me. In a Volkswagen.

"Of course I made it. I have a ticket. We planned this in September."

Had she really thought I just wouldn't show up? Probably. Claire was extremely competitive. This was most likely one more way she wanted to win. I have a boyfriend. He's big and strong and good looking...and present.

Fine. Whatever.

I turned toward the very large man and smiled. "You must be Marcus. We've heard some great things about you. I'm so glad you could make it out for New Year's."

"Sarah." Marcus tried to offer his hand, but Claire wasn't letting go long enough for a casual handshake. "I'm glad you could make it."

"Why wouldn't I have?" I kept my voice sweet and my smile a tad bit confused.

"I...ah..." Marcus glanced at Claire, looking for some help. "I'd heard you might not be feeling well tonight."

"Just tonight?"

"Well..." Okay, so Marcus wasn't the quickest on his feet.

And Claire was letting him take all the heat for doing what she would have done anyway. Only crueler. She should just wear the Dalmatian fur coat and get it over with.

"So, where's the mystery man?"

There it was. Cutting to the chase. I was surprised she lasted that long.

"He's not here." I smiled, daring her to push. Daring her to paint me into the corner we both knew I was in. Daring her to step out on that branch and say, *Yes. I am that much of a bitch.*

"Where is he?"

Okay, so I really shouldn't have been surprised.

"Claire, there's something I want to say to you, and I want you to listen very closely because if someone *has* said this to you before you weren't listening. You're not a very nice person. Actually, you're a petty, mean-spirited person. I'm not sure why you feel the need to compete with everyone. But being on top all the time means you're making sure someone else is on the bottom. So, would it matter if I got dumped on the way over here? Or if he had already had plans for tonight and wanted to hang with his guys. Or if I'd lied because you made me feel bad?"

Claire looked at me as if I were speaking a different language. Maybe this was the first time anyone had made her see how she treated people and how it made them feel. Maybe I should have just said this to her months ago and everything would have been fine. She just needed to know she didn't need to win at everything to be well liked.

Maybe she just needed to hear that.

"What I'm saying, Claire, is life—friendships—aren't a competition. You don't need to *win* to be well-liked."

I felt better already. It wasn't like I was the only one she treated like this. It was going to be good for Becca and Angie too. Maybe I'd feel more comfortable being good friends with those two once Claire chilled out a bit.

"I knew it. There's no mystery guy. You lied. You're such a loser."

"Wow. Claire. I feel really bad for you." I glanced at Marcus, the poor man looking like he wanted to be anywhere but here. Having a guy—even the one you wanted—obviously couldn't fill up an unhappy person.

I stepped out of line, no longer caring about the drink and turned to find table eight—otherwise known as The Most Uncomfortable Seating Plan of the New Year—and walked directly into a man in a twenties broad-striped suit.

"Oh, excuse me." I glanced up, about to dart around him.

"No problem, doll face."

"John! What are you doing here?"

"Just now, I was listening to you tell that woman off. I've never seen you so feisty. You should do that more often.

Now, I'm about to hand you this glass of champagne and ask you to dance."

Oh. Oh this was bad. So very bad. I was doomed. I was more than doomed. I was emotionally apocalyptic.

The first sign was that I couldn't get myself to stop smiling at him. The second was the rush of heat down my entire body just from standing this close to him. The third…Wow. Did he look good in gangster garb or what?

"Who are you?" Claire. Leave it to Claire to ruin a moment.

John hooked his arm over my shoulder and turned me back to face her.

"I'm John. Or you can just continue to call me the Mystery Man if it's easier to remember." He gave her one of his very kind, very soft smiles. If there was anyone who could win Claire over, it was him.

"So, what? Did she hire you or something?"

"Claire." Marcus had shaken her free and was giving her what could only be a stern look.

I think I liked him.

"I met Sarah just after Thanksgiving. She came into my shop. I bought her a coffee. And we've been seeing each other a couple times a week since." Wow. He was good at that not-lying-but-not-quite-telling-the-truth thing. "Now, if you'll excuse us. I'd hoped to get her on the dance floor before the dinner started."

He drew me away, his arm still warm across the back of my shoulders.

He took my drink as we passed table eight and set it down. Taking my hand, he led me out to the floor and then spun me out and back into his arms. I almost melted against him, but I had to remember, this wasn't real. I couldn't give myself away.

Instead, I winked up at him. "My hero."

"You know it, toots." John winked back, always one to be in on the conspiracy—I mean, joke. "A guy's gotta watch out for his dame."

"But, really, what are you doing here?"

"Did you really think I'd let you face the dragon alone? I knew what tonight meant and I hated the idea of you having to deal with her all night. I hate it even more now that I met her. What are you doing hanging out with that woman?"

"It's the Last Single Girl Syndrome."

"It's stupid."

I wanted to tell him I wasn't stupid, but before I could, he'd done some fancy footwork and had us moving around the dance floor like we owned it.

"And before you start lecturing me about girls and friends and that you're not stupid, I agree. With the last one at least. But that Claire woman has some issues. You're better off without her."

"I completely agree. But I'm glad you came and rescued me so I could just enjoy the night." I ducked under his arm as he did another fancy spin thing. "I think you'll like Becca and Angie a lot more. Especially Becca. She's really sweet."

"They need a new C. Maybe you could change your name to Cara and take on the leadership role."

"Or, maybe not."

John just smiled and—like every other time—it made me relax.

"So, back to the 'what are you doing here' part."

He pulled me a bit closer to evade another couple who obviously didn't have the floor skills he did.

"Sorry, mate." The guy winked at us. "You know what it's like, distracted by such a beautiful woman in your arms. Right, sugar?"

The girl just rolled her eyes and away they went.

"Ohhh. Do you think they were actors?"

"There are actors here?" John glanced around suspiciously. "They'll let anyone into these speakeasies nowadays. Next thing you know, coppers will be whispering passwords."

I snorted. John was way more fun than the girls. You had to know Claire was dressed for the night, but wouldn't be playing along.

"Anyway, I kept thinking you'd ask me to go. But when you said you didn't want to bring a fake boyfriend, I knew you weren't going to. I knew you thought you had to do this on your own. But—" He swung me wide around another corner of the dance floor. "How much more fun is this? Thus my very dapper outfit."

"You do look dapper."

"It was quite the adventure getting this. I had to order it online."

One more win for the internet.

"So, why didn't you?"

Why didn't I ask John to be my date? Maybe because I was a complete idiot and didn't realize till the last minute he was perfect for me and then it was too late to ask him casually and too scary to ask him for real?

Or...

"I didn't want to put you out. You've been dealing with my craziness for a month. What if you didn't want to go with me? You'd have said yes anyway because you're so nice."

He mumbled something that sounded suspiciously like *not that nice* and spun me into another turn. "I would have come."

"You *did* come. I can't tell you how glad I am you're here." I tensed. Too much? Could he hear what I really meant?

"I'm glad too. I can't imagine you dealing with that all night."

"To be honest, I was pretty much done with it. I said my piece and if *winning* mattered that much to her, who cares? I was just going to ignore her and enjoy the night and never hang out with her again." The song slowed to an end and John spun me once more and ended us on a dip. "But, I have to say, having you here is so much more fun."

He lifted me back up and gave me another wink. "I know."

Sliding his hand into mine, we headed back to our table, catching the seats facing away from the DJ since we were the last ones there. Claire gave me a smug smile about that as well.

I hadn't realized how tense I was till John shifted his chair over and moved mine so I could lean against him to watch the game introductions behind us. The actors had apparently been there all night. Some of them were wait staff. Some were other guests. Some hadn't shown up yet. Everything was suspect.

The first murder happened during the salad course...directly behind Claire. The second one happened as they were clearing the main course...while she was in the bathroom. The third murder happened while she was whisper-arguing with Marcus about something.

There was a small joy in her frustration.

"I suppose you're all wondering why I called you here." Dessert was being set out, but the man at the front of the room was so good, he pulled everyone's attention to him. "You know we've had three deaths this evening. Now, I know you don't want to get involved, but let me make this as simple as possible—either you help me find the guilty party, or I call in the paddy wagons and shut this gin joint down. You'll all find under your plates a card for you to fill out letting me know who did it and why. If we make an arrest, you're all free to go. If not, we'll be taking you all downtown for questioning."

Oh. He was good. I got little shivers right before the lights dimmed back down.

I pulled my card out and glanced at it. No hints at all.

"Who do you think did it?" John looked at his card. Also blank.

I'd kind of expected there to be checkboxes to pick from, but these guys were hardcore.

Claire leaned in and whispered in Marcus's ear before grinning at the table. "We totally know who it is."

"Oh!" Becca set her card down and leaned in. "Who?"

"I'm not going to tell you. If you don't know, you're just going to have to guess."

Oh, yes. A fun night out with girlfriends.

John leaned in, his nose brushing at the tip of my fake bob. "Okay, we seriously need to kick her ass. She's on my last nerve."

"I didn't know you had a last nerve."

"Well, you're seeing it. So, who is it not?"

We weeded through the characters and realized the only person who'd been around for everything was the sweet, innocent daughter of the mobster. The one we'd seen dancing earlier who we'd almost bumped into.

"Wasn't she dancing with the first dead guy?"

"That's right. And he called her sugar."

"Do you think she killed him?"

"Why not. Jealous lover rage and a cover up? Maybe he was cheating on her with the woman who was killed next."

"Ohhhhh..." I liked how he thought. "Write that down. And what about the third one? He handed the woman the drink. Maybe he knew who poisoned her, so the daughter had to kill him off."

"Brilliant." John scratched it all down and handed our slip to the waiter.

The rest of the table finished theirs and handed them off. Becca, Angie, and John immediately started comparing notes as Claire sat off refusing to share.

"But we already put ours in. We can't change it." Becca always saw the best in everyone, even Claire. She'd assume Claire just didn't understand.

But Claire wasn't willing to share, and really, who cared? No one. Everyone else was enjoying the game and the brilliant chocolate cake with hazelnut ice cream and the company.

"Gents, ladies, I believe I've solved the crime. But it wasn't without your assistance. We have some really smart people in here. Maybe even fed level." He went on to explain that several people had gotten the answer right and they'd drawn winners for a dinner at the house's wine and cheese festival in a few weeks. "And the inspectors are, Sarah and John. Without them we never would have known Rosebud had killed Billy because he was cheating on her with Dolly. And that Sammy the Gun had poisoned Dolly then turned on Rosebud, who shot him. But we've got her in cuffs now folks, so there's no need to worry. Sarah and John, why don't you come up here and let us thank you properly?"

"You won!" Becca bounced in her chair. "That's so cool. I can't believe you guys came up with that."

John took my hand and led me to the front of the room. The detective gave us a bottle of champagne and a gift certificate for the dinner. I stood there grinning like an idiot, my hand clutching John's. When we got back to the table, John waved a waiter over to pop our bubbly.

"Looks like they gave us the good stuff. Perfect for a New Year's Eve toast." He stood and filled everyone's glasses, even Claire's and Marcus's. "To a new year and new friends." He smiled at Becca and Angie. "And to the best New Year's Eve party I've been to in a long time."

Just as we clinked glasses, the big countdown started. I'd planned to be in the ladies room…hiding. How was I going to get through this, that New Year's Eve kiss thing? John pulled me to my feet as everyone else jumped up, wrapping an arm around me and pulling me to him, the warmth of his hand sweeping above the top of my dress, scattering goosebumps across my skin.

"Three…Two…One…Happy New Year!"

Balloons fell from the sky.

Confetti flew threw the air.

People shouted all around us.

I stared up into those soft brown eyes and wanted nothing more than to go up on my tip toes and kiss him. Kiss him for all I was worth and hope it was enough. John's head dipped closer, his eyes slipping shut, as he brushed a kiss across my cheek.

"Happy New Year, Sarah."

FIFTEEN

DATING TRUTH #10: Not every Happily Ever After looks the same.

I SUCKED IN A DEEP breath and reapplied my Berry Dew lip gloss—which was obviously a total waste tonight. I was going to need to come up with a Survive Being In Love With John plan. It wasn't going to be easy. He'd become one of my best friends and favorite people. And it looked like that was all he was ever going to be.

eLove would have to find me Mr. Right after all. Just not until the gooshy place my heart used to be was all patched up.

Back at the table, people gathered their coats and bags, talking about the night and laughing at some of the guesses people had come up with.

"We need to do this again." Becca smiled at everyone, sweet dear. "John, you'll have to close up shop one night to come out and play again. Or maybe we could all just come to you."

Oh, dear stars. This was going to get ugly—or sad and depressing. Or both. I was already trying to figure out how I was going to live through the Wine & Cheese thing—let alone the rest of tonight.

"Name the date, and I'm there." John leaned down and gave tiny, little Becca a kiss on the check.

Look at him just handing those cheek-kisses out like they were candy.

John held out my wrap. As I shrugged into it, he ran his hand down my arm and clasped my hand. I smiled up at him, trying not to be all girly and start crying. This was *John*. Sweet, smart, funny, thoughtful, rescues-me-from-my-own-absurdity, John.

Tears would just be a red flag to his soft soul.

"Ready to go?"

"Um, yes?" I wasn't sure where we were going. Was he going to fake going home with me? That was definitely above and beyond the call of duty. Of course, the whole darn night was the definition of above and beyond.

John waved to the group and pulled me along, my hand still wrapped in his.

"The door guy said they have a deal with a cab company. We should be able to get one pretty quickly."

"Great."

John glanced down at me. The tone of my voice must have put *not so* in front of the *great*. I offered him up a smile, trying to move things along.

Luckily there was one cab left when we got to the portico. John opened the door and I slid in, only half-surprised when he joined me as I gave the driver my address. The driver asked lots of questions about our night and our outfits and whodunit. He seemed thrilled to hear we'd won, like we'd become local celebrities.

I listened with half an ear, trying to mmhmmm in the right places. When we pulled up in front of my condo, John paid the man and slid out behind me, not asking him to wait.

I have never felt so awkward in my life. So divided. I didn't want him to leave. I wanted to just keep being with him, enjoying that smile and humor. But what I really, really needed was to just be alone for a little while.

"Did you want to come up?"

"No." He grasped my hand again, sliding his fingers between mine and giving them a squeeze. "I was just going to walk you to your door and head home."

"Oh. Okay." Wow, well said, Sarah.

At the front door, John pulled my hand, forcing me to turn me to face him.

"I had a lot of fun tonight. Your friends are great. I really do like Becca and her guy."

"Yeah. He was surprisingly nice. I was a little nervous about the whole met-on-a-plane thing. And she's so sweet, I wouldn't want to see her end up with someone taking advantage of that sweetness. I mean, she's just so able to like everyone. She even likes Claire. Not that Claire is horrible. She just has this ridiculous competitive streak that seems to really come out around me. And she's never mean to Becca. Kind of almost mothering sometimes. So, I guess that explains that. Angie is the one who—"

"Sarah."

"—hardest to peg down. She's the one who balances them ou—"

"Sarah."

"—and keeps the peace."

"Sarah."

"I mean—"

John's hand rose and wrapped around my cheek, pulling me up toward him as his mouth settled over mine. His kiss was everything I'd want in the perfect kiss. More powerful than I'd expected from him. Where I'd thought his kiss would be sweet and soft and comfortable, it was powerful and strong—overwhelmingly so. I felt it down to my toes and then back up to my knees just as they gave out. His other arm came around my waist and held me to him, keeping me there in his warmth as if I'd try to escape.

Slowly, with little brushes across my lips and down my jaw, he backed away. Still holding me to him, he blinked.

"Sarah—"

"I—"

"Don't start babbling again. As endearing as it is, I need to get this said." He brushed my hair back out of my face, that soft smile lying about what those lips could really do. "I don't want you dating anyone else. Not at The Brew, not anywhere else. This isn't about you being the last single girl—unless it's about being *my* last single girl. I've been trying really hard for weeks not to throw out every single man who walked through the door. I'd been considering implementing a policy that if you weren't accompanied by a woman, you weren't allowed in."

"Oh." That was perfect. But…"Who's sweetheart? The girl you talk to on the phone?"

John looked confused a moment before he started laughing. "Sweetheart would be my goddaughter, Emmi. Emmi calls me weekly to tell me about kindergarten."

"Emmi?"

"Right. Emmi. Goddaughter." He brushed another kiss across my cheek. "You've driven me to insanity. And I kept waiting—hoping—you'd come in one day and say, *John, I don't want to date any of these eLove guys.* I realize after watching a parade of tall, wealthy suits that I'm not your type, but I want to date you. I don't want you dating anyone else."

He stopped and gave me that *look*. That look he gave me when I was doing something he thought was going to get me in trouble. I couldn't help but wonder if he thought dating him would get me in trouble.

I looked up into those brown eyes, the crinkles in the corner etching out as he looked down at me.

"Well?"

"Well, I *was* worried about being the last single girl…"

"Sarah, I'm not joking."

"I…" I was trying so hard to play it cool, but I had no idea what someone who was playing it cool said when they were being offered exactly what they wanted. "When you walked in tonight, I was more than relieved. I was ecstatic. But I thought you were seeing someone. And before that, I didn't know…I'd been miserable thinking about seeing you again and having to just be friends. I was already coming up with reasons—"

His mouth came down on mine again, softer this time, less urgent, but still so, so very sweet.

"Again with the babbling."

"Babbling equals kiss. I'll keep that in mind." I grinned, too happy to do anything else. "Did you know that in the twenties, the art deco movement that was so popular here actually originated in France when—"

That's as far as I got before he kissed me again.

~*~

Bonus Short Story

It's in His
Kiss

By Bria Quinlan

ONE

THE THICK SMOKER-VOICE ON the other end of the phone made demands I wanted to ignore. "It's time for Chloe's first kiss."

"What? It can't be," I replied, pushing back the panic. "She's far too young to be involved with boys."

"Honey, she's sixteen. Almost seventeen if I remember correctly."

"But, kissing? Boys?" I shook my head against the receiver, my glasses clinking the earpiece. "I don't think she's ready."

"No, Jenna. *You're* not ready. But that doesn't mean a teenaged girl doesn't reach that point without us."

I glared at my Hello Kitty phone, tempted to hang up and claim a bad connection.

"I think maybe a big school dance storyline would be great," Ely continued. "She's co-captain of her soccer team and vice president of the junior class. Isn't there anyone she'd be interested in?"

Ely Morgan, Agent Extraordinaire-slash-Pushiest-Woman-on-the-Planet, had never steered me wrong before—except maybe that one time with the now infamous author-photo-from-you-know-where—but still, good advice was there to be had. That didn't mean I had to like it.

I collapsed back in my worn leather office chair, tempted to spin until I was dizzy. "It's time?"

"Sugar, it's past time."

"I'm not sure." *It's too soon.* "Maybe I could work a potential love interest into the next book." *If anyone good enough crosses my word-processing fingers.* "And then we can fold it into senior year." *Or college. Or never.*

"I know you want to protect her, sweetie." Ely's voice sounded muffled, the click-clack of a keyboard echoing in the background. Agent Extraordinaire was also Multitasking Empress.

The clatter from her phone hitting the ground told me I'd been right.

"Sorry about that," Ely said. "You still there?"

"*Mmhmm.*"

"Okay, Jenna. Here's the deal. Forest Oak won't take another book unless Chloe matures a little. Your fan mail is from girls who grew up with her and, while a lot of them are shy or nerdy or untrusting or whatever it is keeping *them* from kissing a boy, that doesn't mean they don't want Chloe to. So the deal is, next book, out early fall, homecoming maybe. Chloe gets a kiss."

I pushed back and spun, the phone cord wrapping around my neck. A sign, perhaps?

"All right. I'll do my best."

"You always do, my little overachiever."

Without a goodbye, Ely had hung up and gone on to her next seven multitasking events.

Untangling myself from Ms. Kitty's tail, I opened the drawer where my writing notes were lovingly filed, alphabetized and color coordinated. The blue boy file was right where it was supposed to be, fourth back in the character notes, behind the pink girl folder but in front of the black folder of death—the place characters who didn't work out went to die.

Marty O'Donnell — snob, dated best friend, dumped her for an underclassman…er, underclasswoman? Girl?

Mark Andersen — smelled funny, mentioned in three books.

Tony Baccio — funny, smart, cute. Friend's brother. Should be in college this fall.

Kevin Kline — currently dating best friend.

Slamming the blue folder closed, I considered transferring Chloe to a girls' boarding school run by nuns on an uncharted island. If I did that, I could add the blue folder to the black one and cut down on folders. It was economical. It made sense.

It would lose me a contract.

Grabbing Hello Kitty, I dialed Lisbeth Nardi's number in desperation.

"Ciao."

Lisbeth was the only person I knew who could get away with answering her phone like that. She was also the only one I knew who had kissed half the metro area.

"Lis, I need my character to get kissed. I need a guy and a kiss description."

"Aren't you supposed to write what you know?" I heard the laughter in her voice and knew she didn't mean to be cruel. Unfortunately, she was also right.

"That's why I need you. You can tell me how kissing a guy feels the first time." Her earlier words still stung, so I added, "You've had plenty of experience in the first kiss department."

A sigh blasted my ear. One of those declare-yourself-a-martyr sighs.

"First off Jenna, I think what you need to do is just get out there. Get your own first kisses. Get your own life."

I could almost hear her shrug over the phone.

"Second, your character isn't you. Her boyfriend is *imaginary*. He's not going to convince her to go to the same college, propose the middle of junior year, stand her up at the altar because his frat brothers called him an idiot at the bachelor party the night before, and then try to convince her they should still have sex on the side. That stuff only happens to you."

That was painful. True, but painful. And kind of rude. Okay, more than kind of, but I was feeling desperate.

"You're no help." If the queen of the pick-up couldn't help me, I was out of luck.

"Oh, I'll help all right," she answered. "Actually, I wouldn't miss this for the world. Meet me outside O'Leary's at ten and I'll be more help than you could have wished for."

TWO

“WHAT IS THAT?” I ASKED as Lisbeth stepped from the cab.

“What is what?”

“That outfit.”

“Oh, this?” Lisbeth waved a hand in front of the sackcloth she was trying to pass off as a dress. “Cloak of invisibility.”

Sometimes her logic was so…*um*…different that I struggled to follow it, let alone understand it. “I don’t mean to start one of those conversations where we repeat everything the other person says, but, *cloak of invisibility?*”

She adjusted the loose fitting fabric on her shoulders. “Last night, Jeremy said he never would have asked me out if I didn’t have such a, and I quote, ‘hot little body only a bimbo should possess.’ I’m a senior marketing consultant at a huge company and he dated me to get it on with my body.”

“And so you’re hiding it to date men who are only interested in your mind?”

She nodded. I doubted she was unaware of her beautiful face with flawless hair and make-up. Below the short, loose dress stuck out perfectly shaped legs leading down to—

"What the hell are those?" I waved at her clunker-shod feet.

Lisbeth shrugged. "They match the cloak of invisibility."

"Where did you get them?" There's no way she paid money for those. Well, maybe if they had a brand name I couldn't pronounce and a three-digit price tag.

She pointed a toe, still looking dainty in the black, female version of steel toe boots. "I think you left them at my house."

I fought the urge to roll my eyes before I realized it might be true. "You can't really expect to go out wearing that?"

"Oh, like you're one to talk Miss I'm-Dressed-Like-Our-Waiter."

"What?" I glanced down at myself, somehow unsurprised I'd ended up not even knowing what I'd put on. "Darn it."

"My dress doesn't look so bad now, does it?" There was that smug thing again. Why could I never pull off smug? Or look like that in a sack dress.

Or a cocktail gown.

"I put on the black capris and a pink top, but the pink top needed to be ironed." Actually, just about everything I owned needed to be ironed. Always. "So I put on the white top with a navy skirt, but it was too snug. Then I tried that grey dress, but it looked too 'librarians gone bad' for a bar. So I just put on the two most comfortable things and left the house."

Lisbeth smirked as only a gorgeous woman could. Slightly arrogant, yet still gorgeous. "Nothing screams 'can I take your order' quite like a white button-down, short sleeve shirt and black pants."

"Can we just do this?" I pushed. Not that I wanted to head into one of those underlit-overheated holes, but getting it over with was a plus. Glancing at her outfit, I added, "We should stop at an ATM. You might have to pay a cover and buy your own drinks."

Lisbeth got that look you'd give a child who said something stupid but was still adorable.

"No, sweetie. I'll leave that up to you." She grinned and I knew, even dressed like that, she'd be surrounded by men all night. Most of them drooling.

She'd probably even start a new fashion trend.

The doorman took my money and waved me along, but stopped Lisbeth. "ID, miss?"

"Are you kidding me?" I craned my neck to look past the bald, oversized bouncer's head. "Do you really think she could possibly be under twenty-one? She's four years older than I am."

The giant peered over his shoulder. "Do we have a problem, ma'am?"

Cringing at the word ma'am, I snapped, "No. I'm used to it. Go on, Lisbeth. Giggle for the nice man."

Lisbeth shot a look of pure venom my way, making her appear every minute the four years she had on me. I hovered between the door and bar area, waiting for her to finish her flirt-for-entry routine. Eventually, several men turned and stared, the drool almost visible from across the room. Obviously, she'd finally been allowed in.

"I chose this place very carefully." Lisbeth took my arm and steered me toward the bar in the center of the room.

"The men are older, no frat boys. All nice, successful businessmen, rolling up their sleeves at the end of a hard day's work. Even you should be able to handle this."

I placed my handy-dandy notebook on the bar as I climbed atop my stool, making sure not to topple myself onto the already beer-dampened floor.

"Thanks," I mumbled.

Lisbeth beamed, oblivious to the sarcasm. "No problem."

The bartenders were obviously hired for appearance, not ability. The upside was that *Bran* could have graced the seven-foot tall poster outside Abercrombie and Fitch.

"What can I get you ladies?" I liked him immediately. He may have looked only at Lisbeth, but he included me in the question. Very impressive skills at noticing shadows.

"Green Apple Martinis."

"And a Diet Coke," I added.

"I don't think so." Lisbeth turned her smile on the bartender. "Two Green Apple Martinis."

I slid my pen and notebook out of my bag and jotted that down. "Green. Apple. Martini."

"What are you doing?"

"Noting our drinks."

"You write YA. You can't even get your heroine her first kiss. What do you need to know about adult beverages for?"

"Someday I may want to write about this. You know, going out on the town with my friend dressed as Raggedy Anne. Having a couple of drinks. Scoping out guys to hit on in a not-hitting-on-them type of way."

"Who would read that?" Lisbeth squinted at my notebook, the consultant in her running through possible business strategies.

"How would I know? I write YA."

The bartender returned with the order: two Green Apple Martinis…and a killer smile for Lisbeth.

"You might try slouching a little." I honestly was trying to help. If she didn't want attention, I was the girl to show her how to not get it. "Looks lazy and hides those boobs."

Not only did she not slouch, I swear her shoulders went back. "Sweetheart, nothing can hide these girls."

She was right. Or perhaps comparison made hers look so big. Next to my not-quite-B cups, anything needing support was impressive.

Studying the room over her martini, Lisbeth jumped right in. "Scoping the guys is a big part of any night out. Start with looks. There are three categories of guys."

Finally. Something I could answer. "Blond, brunette, redhead."

Her look questioned my almost perfect SAT scores.

"No. Jeep, Civic, Yugo. Obviously you want to avoid Yugos at all cost."

"Obviously." Note: more sarcasm.

"The Jeep is the hot guy. The one that always looks good. And just like his namesake, looks even better with his top off."

"Are you serious?" If this is what I was going to learn out in 'the real world,' no wonder I stayed home so often.

"The Honda," Lisbeth steamrolled my question. She motioned to my notebook with a pointed look until I raised my pen to capture her…um…brilliance. "Is a nice run of the mill guy. Depending on the year and model, he could be close to a Jeep or, you know, more like a rust heap. The Yugo, well, that's self-explanatory."

"And probably what I'll end up with."

"Jenna, you're a solid, one-to-three year off the lot Civic. I'd say you're silver. If you put makeup on, you might even be red. Don't sell yourself short."

So where did that leave me? I was dependable, flat-chested, shopped at the Gap, and you could get me drunk off one drink. Yup, I was a mid-level Honda all right.

I looked at my friend, the Jeep, and counted all the blessings of being a Civic. Low cost, reliable, compact, inexpensive maintenance, low gas mileage.

"So, I need a Civic, right?"

Lisbeth scanned the room, weeding out guys in her head like a chef tossing soft vegetables.

"Him."

Almost directly across the bar sat The Target.

Plusses:

Good looking, but not too good looking

Not wearing a t-shirt or ten-year-old fraternity paraphernalia

Alone. No buddies to face as I made my notations

Lisbeth adjusted herself on the barstool to block the man trying to get her attention. "You can do this. Just be yourse—" Her gaze dropped to my notebook. "Just relax, and smile."

"I can do this." I nodded my head in self-affirmation.

I pictured myself walking around the bar without tripping. I pictured approaching him and no one stepping in front of me. I pictured him turning and smiling at me as I set my drink down without spilling it on him. I pictured him being sweet and understanding and agreeing that, of course it was necessary to research a fictional seventeen-year-old's first kiss in a downtown bar.

"Maybe you should leave that here." Lisbeth took my drink. "You can't even keep milk in a sealed carton."

Every part of me wished she wasn't right, but I left the drink where she placed it. I rounded the bar, no tripping, no bumping, no spilling. First mental picture, completed.

I reached Target Guy's side. My hands shook like a coatless club girl's in a January bar line. Second mental picture, completed.

"Hi." That was easier than expected. Guys complain about having to cross the room all the time.

"I've already got a drink, thanks." Target Guy turned back to the bar.

"I'm not actually a waitress. I'm a writer." I waved my pen and notebook in front of him like a B-movie cop with his badge. "I write YA, ah, young adult. And I'm doing some research."

"In a bar?" While it wasn't an encouraging question, it did give me my in.

"You see, Chloe, my main character, just turned seventeen. Now the publishing house says it's time for her to get a boyfriend. They told Ely, my agent, the next book has to have a boy and a kiss. I disagree, but if I want to continue being paid, it's boyfriend time for Chloe." I laughed, trying to fill the awkward silence before storming forward again. "Which, of course, I worry about. I mean, I *know* she's imaginary, but I feel very protective of her."

I glanced across the bar at Lisbeth and the man sitting in my vacated seat. She gave me the keep going look.

"So, anyway," I continued. "It's been a long time since my first kiss. I'm not sure I could imagine it. I mean, can you even remember your first kiss? I don't mean like who it was with, but like, what was it like, how did it feel. That kind of stuff. So I was wondering if, maybe, you would consider, perhaps, kissing me and I could think about what it would be like being a first kiss of sorts and, if you don't mind, I'd just make some notes."

Target Guy looked dumbstruck. It's a common expression, but this was the first time I'd seen it in action. Or, as the case may be, *in*action.

"Make some notes?"

Encouraged, I nodded and waved my handy notebook again to reassure him. "Yeah. I'm not some crazy pick-up girl. I just need to make some notes."

I kept expecting the dumbstruck look to go away.

"Are you ordering another drink?"

The look stayed as he turned toward the new voice.

"I'm not a waitress," I explained to the petite woman who appeared at my side.

"Sorry. Are you a friend from work? I'm Jamie, Mike's girlfriend."

"Oh." I could feel the heat creeping toward my cheeks, starting at the edge of my waitress-wannabe-white shirt, past my neck and up to my ears. "Girlfriend. I'm so sorry. I wasn't hitting on him. I'm just doing research for a book."

"Wow, a book. What do you write?" Jamie asked.

"Young adult. I write about a teenage girl named Chloe."

Jamie pulled her stool out as she asked, "What kind of research are you doing here?"

"Okay. I think we have to go." Mike jumped off his stool. "It was very, ah…nice, to meet you. We have a reservation. I'm sure we don't want to miss our table."

He had Jamie by the arm and was pulling her away under protest. "But our reservation isn't for forty minutes."

By the time Mike responded, the couple was safely at the door. He glanced over his shoulder, still slightly dumbstruck, as he pushed his girlfriend out into the street. She, sweet girlfriend girl, gave me a little half-shrug and waved as the door swung shut.

Men were supposed to be easy. They weren't supposed to get embarrassed by a woman wanting to kiss them.

NOTE: *Although prone to stating embarrassing things in public, men seem to be easily embarrassed by forward-thinking women.*

EXAMPLE: *Mike at the bar, who was too embarrassed to tell his girlfriend about being asked for a kiss. This statement would not have reflected poorly on him, so why be embarrassed?*

I set my notebook on the bar and contemplated the fact I might not be the type of girl to pick up a guy in a bar—or even to not-really-pick him up. Also, the fact we were in a bar was probably irrelevant.

Beyond the chair Mike had sat in, a pair of broad shoulders hunched over the bar and pulled at my awareness. It wasn't the broadness of said shoulders that demanded attention, but their shaking. Dark hair with threads of auburn flopped over his forehead. He hid his face in his hands, elbows propped up on the bar.

Poor thing. To be weeping so openly in public. Some girl must have really ripped his heart out and carted it out the door with her. Pushing Mike's chair out of the way, I slid over to the stranger. I laid a hand on his arm and softened my voice so no one else would hear.

"It's okay. I'm sure whatever she said to you couldn't be half as bad as it sounded."

The shoulders shook harder and then slowly—so slowly—the dark head rose. Pink rimmed from crying, his chocolate eyes studied me a moment before the sound burst forth from his mouth.

The jerk! He wasn't crying. He was laughing. At me.

THREE

R EJECTED AND RIDICULED, I PIVOTED to leave the heckler alone at the bar where I'd found him. Where he deserved to be. In typical Jenna form, my sleeve caught on the arm of the empty stool, tipping it over and tripping me up. An annoyingly strong arm caught me around the waist and lifted me away from the wreckage before I joined it on the beer-soaked floor.

"Whoa there," a voice rumbled behind me, his chest reverberating against my back as he held in the laughter.

He was taller than he looked slumped over the bar. My head brushed under his chin as he lifted me over the stool and set me down. His hands slid around to rest on my hips as if he were afraid I'd spontaneously fall over if he let go.

I probably would have.

"Now," the voice re-rumbled. "Why don't you explain to me what you and your little notebook are doing in this bar."

The hands fell away and I turned, my nose almost brushing his crisp, button-down shirt.

It was truly unfortunate. If Lisbeth had said, describe your dream man, I would have—without a doubt—described Mocking Guy, without having ever seen him before.

Tall enough to wear heels with. Dark hair flopping over wire rimmed glasses. White button-down sleeves rolled and tucked into jeans tight enough to look good and loose enough to, well, look good.

I glanced at the barstool lying on the floor and considered picking it up, but bending over in a bar seemed like a bad idea unless I was looking to get my butt smacked.

"Okay. Well, thanks." I stepped over the stool, making sure each foot cleared by at least a clean inch, when a warm hand clamped around my wrist.

"I don't think so, Sunshine." Mocking Guy pulled my notebook from my hand and settled back onto his stool. "This is the closest thing to fun I've had since my friend dragged me in here."

I gaped at him. I mean, I'd written that description before. Teenagers seem to gape a lot, but now, doing it, I felt just plain stupid. Where were all my snappy comebacks? Obviously I needed someone to follow me and do instant re-writes on my personal scenes.

In horror, I watched him flip the notebook open and page through to tonight.

"NOTE: Although prone to stating embarrassing things in public, men seem to be easily embarrassed by forward-thinking women." Mocking Guy cocked an eyebrow at me. "Forward-thinking women? Is that what you are?"

Rounding the stool, I came at him from the other side and snatched at my notebook. "Yes. You probably wouldn't understand the concept, but not all women believe they need to do exactly what's expected."

"And yet, I have a feeling that you always do." He smirked and leaned back, crossing his arms over a chest that matched the aforementioned broad shoulders.

"Please give that back." I was horrified at the squeak my voice made and hoped he couldn't hear it over the man warming up with his tin whistle.

"Just a minute." Mocking Guy reached over the bar and snagged a pen. Flipping to the next blank page, he began scribbling, his left hand held out to keep me at bay. Then, with a nod to himself, he flipped the book closed and said, "Okay."

"Okay what? Okay, you've violated my privacy enough? Okay, you wrote something sufficiently mocking? Okay, I can chalk this experience up to 'what not to do in public'?"

"So." His hand wrapped around my wrist and pulled me toward the bar. "Can I buy you that drink now?"

A good-looking guy wanted to buy me a drink at a popular nightspot. There were so many things wrong with that statement I couldn't keep track of them all.

Glancing across the bar, I signaled Lisbeth to rescue me. I expected her to sweep down in all her gorgeousness, distract the arrogant man and allow me to regain my notebook. Instead, the traitor shook her head and motioned for me to do something—probably flirt—with him.

"Listen," he said, forcing my attention back to him. "One drink and you can have your little scratchpad back."

Before I could reach for it, he stood, shoved it in his back pocket and sat back down. How was I ever supposed to write in it again now that it had been rubbing against those jeans I had admired a few minutes ago?

"Listen," I tried to mimic his tone. "Give it back to me and I'll introduce you to Lisbeth. All you had to do was ask nicely."

His whole face went all smirky-smirky and he glanced across the bar where Lisbeth was surrounded by a bevy of male model wannabes and a couple of geeky but successful-looking CEO types.

"So, if I asked nicely, you'd cut me through that herd of followers to introduce me to your friend just to get this notebook back?"

"In a heartbeat." That heartbeat stopped. He was going to ask me to introduce him to Lisbeth. The only guy who'd looked twice at me in six years, even if it was to laugh at me, and he was going to ask what every other guy did.

He eased his back against the bar, his hand still warm around my wrist, and leaned in to whisper over the growing noise of the crowd. "Not a chance, Sunshine."

FOUR

STOP CALLING ME THAT." DEAR God, the man took control of everything, starting with my humiliation and continuing with my name. "I am not your sunshine."

This is the thing I hated most about being Lisbeth's friend. It wasn't the horde that surrounded her.

It was that one-in-a-billion man who got my attention and, even if he was arrogant and overbearing, held it when I knew all he'd want was to walk that beautiful Levi's-covered butt over to see if she'd give him the time of day.

He glanced across the bar, his perusal slow. I could see him take in Lisbeth and knew what he saw. His eyes scanned the crowd around her, the men bantering for her attention, the women shooting her envious looks, the bartender keeping her well-liquefied.

Once, just once, it would have been nice to be the object of that type of study. The kind that takes in everything, weighs the odds and then ignores them to pursue regardless.

"I don't want to deal with dolts vying for attention when I'm wooing a woman." The left side of his mouth quirked up in a lopsided smirk. "It isn't the competition. I just don't like to share."

"So, what exactly do I need to do to get my notebook back?" I eyed his bottom, wondering if I could just reach in his pocket and retrieve it. He really did have a nice butt. Maybe that's what distracted me from grabbing my notebook and gave him time to swing around, that lopsided smirked aimed at me again.

"Here's what I'm thinking." He leaned in as if to tell me the best kept secret outside Julia Robert's anti-wrinkle treatment. "I'll grab my friend. You grab your friend. We'll get out of here before she starts a riot and he starts a bar fight over someone else's girlfriend."

I turned to look at the guy he'd jerked his head toward. If I thought Mocking Guy was hot, his friend was Adonis. Attitude and all.

"And?" It was a good excuse as excuses went to end this public torture. I *had* to leave the bar to get back the notebook I needed in order to write my story. Even Lisbeth couldn't argue with that.

The right side of his mouth quirked up to join the left in a full-ray smile.

"And then we go have some fun." Mocking Guy stood up, patted me on the bottom and said, "Go get your girl. We'll meet you out front."

My rear tingled. Seriously, like shimmery little tingles. I couldn't remember the last time someone had dared to touch any part of me that wasn't a polite handshake. Not that it mattered since he was just warming up his moves for Lisbeth.

Mr. Guy (we should be on first name basis after that bottom-pat, but I liked to keep clear boundaries) cut his way through the crowd, bee-lining for Adonis.

I watched him go. Couldn't help myself. I also watched the girls he passed watch him go. One reached for him as he squeezed between her and a table, her hand resting on his arm as if to test its withheld-power. Mr. Guy bent toward her, his hair flopping forward over his glasses. She, tiny little annoying-perfect thing that she was, went up on tiptoes to whisper in his ear. Mr. Guy threw back his head and laughed.

Must be nice to make him laugh with you, not directly *at* you.

Mr. Guy shook his head and kept moving, inching closer toward Adonis through the crowd. The faery girl turned and scanned the crowd, her gazing landing on me, hardening before she shrugged in a disgusted kind of way.

Yeah. I knew that look. It said "As if." And I knew the answer too: Never. Of course, she sighted me, not Lisbeth. If she knew his real target, she'd back down, claws retracted, without another glance. Instead, I got the death-ray vision look.

Didn't she know sidekicks were benign?

FIVE

S WALLOWING A SIGH, I TRIPPED my way back around
to Lisbeth, pushing through the circle of men to the
epicenter of beauty.

I reached between the remainder of hovering males
between me and the bar to grab her attention. "Lis. We're
leaving."

Grabbing my hand, she brought me through the crowd to
her side. "Gentlemen, this is my friend, Jenna. She's a world
famous writer."

The men all made polite-humor-the-friend noises, their
eyes never straying from Lisbeth.

I leaned in, desperate to get out of there and trade her for
my notebook. Mocking Guy was hot, funny (at my expense),
and intelligent. She wouldn't mind meeting him. I mean, who
would?

"Lisbeth, seriously. We have to go. That guy took my
notebook and he'll give it back if we go hang out with him

and his friend." I struggled not to roll my eyes. "He wants to meet you. He committed theft to do it."

Lisbeth had a serious bad boy addiction and the idea of someone stealing to meet her had her eyes lighting up like a night game at Fenway. My stomach turned over. She was going to like him. She'd seen me talking to him and was already running her flirt-calculations behind those lit-up eyes.

Lisbeth nudged bald-bouncer guy on the way out and we slipped past the line.

"So?" She pulled out a tiny mirror and did a quadrant-by-quadrant check of her hair and make-up.

"So what?" I watched the door to make sure he hadn't convinced me to leave and then left me trapped outside without my notebook. I glanced at Lisbeth.

He'd show.

"So, this guy. He's obviously hot." Lisbeth grinned. "I noticed him sliding glances over the bar at me. Hopefully he's worth more than just getting your notebook back. I'd hate for you to go home without your security blanket."

Sometimes I hated her. It was bad enough she got the guy without even talking to him, but referring to the handy-dandy as a security blanket—well, that was about the end of the night for me.

Sucking in a breath, I did the dance. The one we did every time we went anywhere. Only, I didn't typically feel nauseous as I did it.

"Well, you can see he's hot. He seems smart. He has a sense of humor if you count laughing at me." I ran through our conversation. "Strong. He picked me up with one arm around my waist. Arrogant. He kept thinking if he said something, it must be so. Like buying me a drink and calling me Sunshine as if I'm five or something."

"What does he do?" she asked, shrugging her shoulders so the sackcloth-dress casually fell off one. Geez, how did she do that?

"For work?" Or for fun? Because that would apparently be *torture me*. "I don't know."

"Does he live in town?"

Had we discussed that? "I'm not sure where he lives."

"Well, what's his name at least?"

My gaze flashed back to the door, hoping he'd just walk out and answer the questions for himself. "Mocking Guy. But you can call him Mock."

Lisbeth raised her eyes and studied me. Her words came out slowly, as if she were talking to a very small child. "You don't know his name? You dragged me out here to meet a guy and you don't know all the important stuff?"

"I told you, he's smart, funny, and relatively nice."

"Jenna," she sighed my name. "You know better than that. You've never let a guy through without checking his stats for me before."

And there it was, laid out in vivid HD. The basis of our friendship. I was her gatekeeper. If Mr. Guy hadn't had my notebook, I would have walked away right then.

Lucky for me, Mocking Guy and Adonis chose that moment to exit the bar or I may have said something to kill my chance for handy-dandy retrieval. Even with them nearing I was weighing the odds of being able to re-create the plot points I'd outlined in the notebook.

Mr. Guy's gaze flowed over Lisbeth. I imagined him taking in every inch of well-honed girliness only emphasized by my plain waitress-looking self. His gaze shifted my direction. His lips did that side-quirky smirk thing and my stomach dropped like coming over the top of a roller coaster.

This guy was too hot, too interested in Lisbeth, and too likely to laugh at me, but here I was blushing and on the verge of drooling. I was even stupider than I thought.

So, I'd do the introductions, get them all hooked up, get my notebook, and take off. If I ignored Lisbeth's calls for three, maybe four, days she'd have moved on to the next post-Jeremy guy and I'd be rethinking my life, my friends, and the universe.

Mr. Guy's smirk morphed into that full-ray smile as he turned back to Lisbeth and stuck his hand out.

"Ladies." Mr. Guy nodded one of those *if this were two-hundred years ago it would have been a bow* nods. "I'm Ben. This," he tipped his head to signify Adonis, "is Dane."

Dane took my hand, shaking it lightly in an offhanded way. "And you are?"

The man was gorgeous. Like blindingly, stunningly, overwhelmingly gorgeous. The entire group was in the majors and I was in however many As signified 'can't catch the ball.' I'd forever be proud that I somehow managed to stutter out, "J-Jenna."

Lisbeth held her hand out in that half-turned way that left a person wondering if she expected him to shake it or kiss it. Ben went one better. He took her hand, sparking that smile again, and tucked it in the crook of his elbow.

Lisbeth looked from Ben—the guy who stole to meet her—to Dane—the guy who made George Clooney look dowdy. Before Dane could move away, she wrapped her other hand around his polo-clad bicep. Nudging each away from the club, not to mention me, she asked oh-so-innocently, "So, where's this fun place we're going?"

Ben's head angled toward her, his profile lit by the neon bar lights behind us. His expression wasn't quite as innocent. "You'll just have to wait and see, won't you?"

With a tug, he pulled the little party down the street in front of me, my notebook sticking out of his pocket. Glancing over his shoulder, he had the annoying-hot-guy audacity to wink at me.

I could seriously learn to hate this man.

"Don't worry," Ben tossed over his shoulder. "I'm not that bad."

I slapped a hand over my mouth, surprised and yet not that I'd let slip my thoughts aloud.

The Beauty Brigade continued down the sidewalk in front of me, comfortable enough with their place in the world to—rudely—walk three across.

Two blocks from the bar, Ben stopped and slid Lisbeth's reluctant hand off his arm. Leaning around her, he jerked his head at Dane, indicating the CVS we'd stopped in front of.

Lisbeth gave them her best pout as the two men asked us to wait outside. Once the doors fell shut behind them, she turned a smirk toward me.

"He's a little too sure of himself, don't you think?" She pulled out the little mirror and reapplied her lipstick.

I wondered who was the too-sure person as I watched her primp for a man she'd just met. Of course, she'd never been wrong before.

"What happened to wanting a guy to want you for more than your body?" I asked.

"Of course he does. I mean, he couldn't want me dressed like this?" She waved at the dress again.

"Lis, you haven't even talked to him. He saw you surrounded by all your admirers and that's that."

Lisbeth tucked her mirror back in her purse. "Just because you don't have men wanting you from across a crowded room, doesn't mean it doesn't happen to the rest of us."

Okay, so now it wasn't just her, it was all womenkind I was less attractive than. Lovely.

The guys came through the automatic doors and Ben's gaze narrowed. Did he catch the way Lisbeth's eyes grew round and sultry instead of narrow as they swung from me to him? He shook the bag in his hand and led us away. I couldn't help the little internal grin I got from his not offering Lisbeth his arm again.

The music drifting from open club doorways faded as we crossed the street toward the college area. At a dark corner, Ben stopped and faced us.

Giving the CVS bag in his hand another little shake, he said, "We're there."

Lisbeth's nose squished up before she caught herself. "We're where exactly?"

"Disco Ball Bowling Alley."

Pushing open the dark brown door, Ben grinned as the music rushed out over us.

"This is the something fun?" Lisbeth asked.

"This is the something more than fun."

Lisbeth peeked through the door, her hand wrapping around Ben's bicep as she leaned past him. After a moment, she pulled back and cocked an over-arched eyebrow at him.

Seeing that she had zero interest in moving, I took the lead and marched past him through the graffiti covered door. Inside, colors flashed by me off the disco balls scattered about the room, the music rivaling that of a dance club.

"I'm not going in there," Lisbeth shouted through the door at us. "If you think I'm sticking my bare feet in used, public shoes, you're not exactly more than a pretty face."

"I'd never expect you to. These made me think of you." Ben dug around in the CVS bag. With a ridiculously overly showy sweep of his arm, he brought out a little pair of black socks with hearts on them and handed them to her. "And these made me think of you."

The next pair pulled out were Peanut M&M yellow.

"No." I shook my head. "Why does she get little hearts and I get blind-the-crowd yellow?"

"What'd you think you were going to get, Sunshine?"

"A headache." I snatched the socks and marched to the counter, hoping everyone was following me.

"Eight," I said to the teenager at the register before I had a chance to change my mind. Reaching in my bag, I pulled out the money that should have been paying my cab fare away from this mess.

A large hand covered mine before the bills cleared the leather.

"There's four of us. One lane." Ben handed the kid some cash and scooted my shoes toward me. "Go warm up, Sunshine. I don't want any excuses about how badly you're going to lose."

Lose! He'd already stolen my notebook and used me to pick up my friend, there was no way I was letting him beat me at bowling.

I mean, how hard could it be?

I glanced at the little desks in front of each alley. All you had to do was roll a ball and knock down sticks. I could knock down stuff without trying. Heck, I'd taken out that bar stool like it was a straw hut and I was the Big Bad Wolf.

Klutziness was finally going to be my friend. Roar.

SIX

I STOOD THERE, NOT REALLY SURE what to do with my super-Lysol'd patchwork shoes as Ben slid another pair toward Lisbeth. I'd never seen anyone accept rented footwear like they were some overpriced designer I wouldn't own.

I guess there really was a first time for everything.

"Lane eleven, ladies." Ben cocked his head toward the alleys, pointing toward the far lane, and gave me a little shove. As I turned to go, his size twelves swatted my bottom with a dull thud. "That's the lightest part of the butt kicking I'm going to give you tonight."

I really didn't like him. I mean, good-looking and cocky go together so frequently it's basically a cliché, but he brought it to a whole new level.

At lane eleven—which just happened to be my lucky number so I was feeling hopeful—I dropped onto the bench-seat thing next to Lisbeth. She was already pulling the little metal clasp thing off her new heart covered socks.

"He isn't subtle, is he?" Lisbeth purred…yeah, she purred. "Little hearts. Very cute in a junior-high-check-yes-or-no kind of way, don't you think?"

I would have answered her, I probably would have even told her what she wanted to hear, but my socks weren't as easily parted. They were fastened together with one of those plastic things that looks like a question mark. Ripping them apart didn't work, so I'd had to resort to gnawing through the plastic stem.

"But," she continued, smirking at the fuzzy yellow material hanging from my lips, the ankle pom-poms bouncing about my chin. "What's up with the bright yellow? Is he colorblind or something?"

The stem snapped and my teeth slammed together with an inner-ear shattering clank. He had literally driven me to gnashing my teeth. What did this say about him? Nothing good. He'd probably be the perfect match for Lisbeth.

I glanced over my shoulder, wondering what had happened to Ben and Dane. They were still at the counter talking to a guy in a white t-shirt with greased back hair. I had a little John Travolta flash, but then the music hit me. Okay, actually the hem of the poodle skirt of the girl who was roller skating by hit me. Either way, I glanced around suddenly afraid that we had been sucked into a fate even worse than Disco Bowling.

60's Themed Disco Bowling.

Which, let's stop and just consider the oddity of anything that has "60's" and "Disco" in the same phrase…

Not needing any more mocking than strictly necessary, I covered my new yellow socks with those foot-slut shoes.

As the guys joined us, the music ended with a staticky click and the gates at the end of all the lanes dropped. Before I could look for the red emergency exit lights, Elvis's *I Can't Help Falling In Love With You* filled the silence, and a spotlight lit the end of our alley. The greased-back hair guy stood there, multi-color mod-skirt girls surrounding him with a swish of over starched crinoline.

Bowling Theater. Who would have guessed.

As I sat back to enjoy the show, Greaser Guy raised the mic and belted out the first bars of the song, little 60's girls swooning about him until he strolled down the alley in our direction. There was no way this could go well for me. With a spotlight and a mic heading my way, I figured I'd probably accidentally maim someone or bring the building down around us.

When the group got to the end of the lane, Greaser Guy gave each girl a good looking over before brushing them off one-by-one. Then, with frightening precision, he turned our way, his grin widening as he studied our group.

Lisbeth perked up, doing that shoulder roll thing again to drop her dress down one arm before flipping her hair back in a move I swear she was considering patenting. I tried to slide my feet under the bench, praying I wouldn't trip him as he threw himself prone before Lisbeth.

Greaser Guy slid around the little score-keeping desk and moved our way, the song still flowing as every eye in the house followed him into our safely-out-of-the-spotlight area.

And then, everything happened in slow motion.

Greaser Guy passed the mic to his other hand and reached our way. Lisbeth, her glossy lips slipping into a pouty smile, lifted her own to allow him to take it...or kiss it...or something. Only, he reached right past her. To me.

He swept my hand from my lap and, with a gentle tug, pulled me to my feet and toward the spotlight. With an over-dramatized sigh, he collapsed to his knees, singing for my eternal love, if not my eternal mortification. And then, as he crooned the last promise of love, the lights went dead.

SEVEN

S THE MUSIC ENDED AND the light dimmed, I
turned to escape back to our group. Before I made
it more than two steps, the singer's hand wrapped
around my upper arm and tugged me back into the lane and
the center of attention.

"Not so fast, miss." He raised the mic and spoke to the
crowd. "I may look like a flashback to a kinder, gentler time,
but I believe women should be as giving with their gifts as
men. And so, I'm going to hand the microphone over to my
lovely partner for the next song."

With a thud, the mic ended up in my hand, the cord
twisting between my feet as he gave me a gentle shove toward
the center of the spotlight. My gaze rose, shooting through
the light and into the darkness beyond to lock onto Ben, the
forever Mocking Guy. His lips curled in a slight grin, a
challenge issued with the mere cocking of his eyebrow.

Beside him, Lisbeth laid a hand on his arm and leaned in
to whisper who-knew-what in his ear. His light grin grew, his

brow dropping as he turned toward her and said nothing. Probably stunned anew by her shabby-chic beauty. Without replying, he settled back on his plastic chair-bench seat and crossed his arms over his chest.

He was really looking forward to watching me fail.

My gaze slid toward Lis, looking for support, looking for my friend. Only I looked too soon. Well, too soon for what I wanted to see.

You know those moments in life when you walk down the street and you glance up and see someone you haven't run into for ages and their expression before their polite-person mask falls into place is not so welcoming? Well, that's what I got. I got that moment. And I saw the ugly side of friendship.

I saw dislike and a hope that I'd fail.

There I was, dragged out of my nice little apartment to pretend to hit on men I had no interest in for her sad version of "research," and now stuck in this warehouse of a bowling alley in a horrible neighborhood that stunk of over boiled hot dogs and stale beer. Trapped in this place because of yet another guy who wanted her and would do stupid things to have her. Not only would she let him, but she'd love every minute of it. And there was no way she'd share the spotlight in a good way…no way unless it was to watch me fail.

I don't *think* so.

We all have a past, things we've put away. And not all of those things are bad. Some are wonderful, wonderful things that just aren't the core that moves our heart as strongly as something else.

But that doesn't mean they aren't part of you anymore.

College had robbed me of something. It had robbed me of part of myself. That wasn't fair. I had given part of myself away to be the girl my high-school-slash-college sweetheart wanted me to be.

As he pledged his fraternity and became one of the Big-Man-On-Campus-In-Trainings, the idea of me being the nerdy girl I'd been in high school was unacceptable. He never said *I* was unacceptable, but I was *more* acceptable not being in choir. Or drama club. Or Latin debate. Yeah, I debated in Latin, you have a problem with that?

And so, those things got put away for the boy who eventually threw me away. But that didn't mean my heart didn't remember them, didn't long for them, didn't long to sing.

My gaze slid back to Ben, looking to see that smirk of his so I could watch it fall from his face when the words slid from my lips in a clear, perfectly pitched melody. The music started—a perky oldies tune—and that's when my confidence slid away instead. Okay, it landslided away, but who was really counting? All I could think was, *It figured.*

I totally blanked on the song.

I knew I should have known it. It was vaguely familiar in the way that kid who moved away in kindergarten was when you saw him again as an adult. But, tune? Not really. Words? Not at all.

I must have shown the panic on my face, because Lisbeth's hand came up to hide what I could only presume was a smirk and Ben leaned forward for what I could only presume was a better view of my humiliation.

The singer must have also seen my panic, because he stepped back into the sphere of shame—I mean the spotlight—and gently turned me toward the place where the scores were typically projected. The words were there in all their glorious 60s-ness. Throwing an arm around me, he whispered in my ear.

"Almost there. 3...2...1..."

And then it all came together. It was like getting halfway through a book and realizing I'd read it before.

The words and the tune were so simple, so easy to grasp, that I was belting it out before I knew what I was saying. What the words were saying. There was no way Ben could have done this to me on purpose, but the coincidence was too great to discount him being in league with Lucifer. I didn't even see it coming until the moment before the chorus flashed on the screen. By then, my memory had caught up with the words. The very ironic words.

About love.

And longing.

And knowing he's the right guy because it's all there...in his kiss.

At this rate, I was going to have a justifiable reason to kill him. Even his mother wouldn't be able to blame me for retaliating against this very public mocking.

There was no way after making me sing about kisses that he was going to keep me from writing about them. As soon as the crowd stopped clapping—okay, they were cheering, so I hammed it up a bit—I was going to demand my notebook back and storm out of this bowling alley like a modern day Scarlett O'Hara.

Never to be mocked again.

Handing the mic back to the guy, I stepped off the brightly lacquered wood. As my eyes adjusted, I saw Lisbeth had put her happy face back on, clapping along with the rest of the group. Smiling as if there hadn't been that moment where she wanted me to fail. I couldn't help but wonder if it had been more than a moment.

Ben stepped forward, his grin a little wider than before, but he was brushed aside as Lisbeth rushed toward me.

"That was awesome," she gushed. "I didn't know you could sing. Why didn't you ever tell me. You...you...hidden talents girl. I never know what you're going to come out with next, *JJ*."

The last word, the initials, were spoken in that sly way someone might say something when they want people to ask about it. When they know the answer and can't wait to share it. When they have bad news or gossip.

"Nice job." Dane reached past Ben to high five me. "What's the JJ stand for?"

I knew it was coming, knew I couldn't escape it, so I figured I might as well just get it over with. The smaller the production made of something, the smaller the deal people thought it was. Usually. I kept my gaze on Dane, not wanting to see the mocking attack coming when I spit it out.

"Jenna Jameson."

Dane's eyes rounded, but he had the good grace not to say anything. My gaze slid toward Lisbeth and there it was again. That pre-mask look of triumph.

But it was Ben who couldn't keep his mouth shut.

"You're named after a porn star?"

EIGHT

I AM *NOT* NAMED AFTER A porn star."

Honestly, you'd think people would get tired of asking that. Okay, so the same people didn't keep asking it, but *everyone* did.

"Not that I'm a porn expert or anything," Ben said. "But I believe Jenna Jameson is not only a porn star, but the most famous one ever. I mean, even my mom's probably heard of her."

I must have given him a look, because he rushed on before I could point out just how weird that was.

"You know what I mean. You know who Heidi Fleiss is too, but that doesn't make you a prostitute."

And I'd thought the conversation couldn't get weirder. Next to me, Dane cleared his throat, his brows raised over the hand covering his mouth. Apparently I wasn't the only one wondering what was going on with Mocking Guy—who was quickly becoming Weirdo Guy. Before things could veer more, I jumped in.

"And, anyway, it's Jenna Drake. Jameson is my middle name," I rushed on when Ben started to turn to Lisbeth for verification. "It was my mom's maiden name."

Ben nodded. Dane nodded. Ben looked at Lisbeth, who began nodding. Yeah, this was an exciting night out, alrighty.

"So, are we going to bowl, or what?" I almost added that the sooner we got this over with, the sooner I could have my notebook back and escape. But that seemed rude even for someone as desperate to leave and socially manipulated into staying as I was.

"Of course." Lisbeth stepped into the center of our small circle. "Why else would we be here?"

She slid a sly grin toward Ben. Yeah, we all knew why we were really here: So she could add another guy to her Ken Doll Collection. Did anyone remember my notebook?

I glanced at my watch. How could it possibly only be 11:09?

"So," Lisbeth continued, stepping up to the edge of the alley. "I'm not much of a bowler. I take it there's some type of form you need to do things right?"

She ran her hand over the ultra-pink ball she'd chosen before hefting it. Turning sideways, she glanced toward us, that grin teasing more than just her lips.

"Are they all this heavy?" she asked as she set it back down and checked her manicure. "That seems a little unfair for the girls."

Dane spun the balls, looking at the numbers carved into them. "Try this one. It should be a little lighter. Sorry it's not pink."

Good Lord, he was gorgeous. When he was being his normal charming self he was lovely, but when he focused that smile on a girl he was absolutely stunning. My heart stopped from collateral shivers. No wonder Lisbeth was working so hard to keep both guys in the game.

"Why don't you guys give me some pointers before we get started?" she asked, and just like that, Lisbeth was back where she liked to be: the center of attention.

She did a replay of that shoulder roll thing that had her sack-dress dropping elegantly off one shoulder. Then, batting her eyelashes with a giggle, Lisbeth gracefully eased her hand back and swung it forward is if to throw an imaginary ball down the alley that was—of course—nowhere near her since she had strategically turned sideways for the greatest viewing angle.

One guy's gaze went right, one left. Well, I guess we now knew who liked legs in the group.

Lisbeth held her pose for a moment before straightening and flipping her hair in her signature move.

Oh for crying out loud. First the guys ask me if I'm named after a porn star and now Lisbeth is acting like a stripper.

"Actually," Ben said, making me wonder what he was replying to. "A stripper takes her clothes off while she makes a spectacle of herself."

Exactly how many 'Did I say that out loud' moment could I squeeze in tonight?

I turned to face him, not even considering letting him off the hook. "Same difference, right? She had your full and undivided attention in a manner that isn't what someone might consider modest. It must be hard to be so easily lead astray."

I peeked in her direction to see what she was up to now. At the head of the alley, Lisbeth grasped the bowling ball between her two tiny hands, Dane rearranging her stance. But he wasn't who had her attention. Ben was.

I'll give Ben this—he was one smart cookie. He'd gotten her game from the beginning and now he gave her just enough attention to keep her working the flirt instead of looking at him like he wasn't good enough to polish her rented shoes. He hovered at my elbow, that cocky grin and lifted eyebrow mocking me...a state of affairs I was depressingly used to in only one hour.

"You know," Ben continued as if he was going to say something I might be interested in. "You don't have to let her grab all the attention like this. I brought Dane to make the numbers nice and even."

Seriously? He brought the most gorgeous man on Earth for me so he'd be free to flirt with my friend?

"You know what you need?" he asked.

It was never a good thing when someone asked that. For years I'd been trying to come up with a way to stop that sentence in its tracks, but I never seemed to find one. Instead of looking lame, I just cocked a brow at him.

"You just need some lessons in flirting." He grinned and I wanted to kick in his perfectly straight, white teeth. "Sunshine, by the end of the night you're going to need that notebook back for all those kissing notes if you listen to me."

NINE

S O THAT WAS HIS GAME!
Commit theft and blackmail to get Lis, then distracting me with the most perfect specimen of male beauty ever seen.

Not so fast, mister.

"So, not only did you steal my notebook to get at Lisbeth, but you're willing to pimp your buddy out to her boring friend?"

His smile slipped a bit. Most guys didn't like being reduced to a Seller-of-People, I guessed.

"That's what you think? That I'd pimp him?" He stepped forward into my dance space.

If I was Baby, I'd be telling this Johnny off. Of course, if I was Baby I'd be secretly having an affair with him while my doctor-daddy totally missed that I'd grown up and become a slummer at the resort.

What was my point? Oh, yeah. Him big pimping and space invading.

"Let's see." I held up my hand and started ticking reasons off on my fingers. I feared I might run out of digits before I got to the end of this particular tirade. "You laugh at my embarrassment. You steal the notebook that you *know* I need for work. You blackmail me so you could meet my friend. You then drag us here, which I can only assume is because you know there's no competition for her attention in a back-alley bowling alley. Then you flirt with her outrageously. But, when you see you need to distract me more, you throw Mr. Too Good Looking To Be Real at me."

His smile thinned, predatory. Like he knew so many things I didn't. Which was probably true. He took another step toward me, forcing me backward.

Over his shoulder, I heard the high pitched giggle of a Lisbeth trying to regain everyone's attention. Sorry Lis, but you're on your own. I had to escape the big bad wolf.

Each step he took toward me, I took one back. His smile became *thicker*, as if I were being hunted and he'd suddenly turned deadly.

My back hit a wall before I'd noticed he'd walked us into the darkened emergency exit.

"I'm flirting with her? You think I'd give her two glances if she wasn't your friend?" His hand came up. "Yeah, I'd give her two glances. But they wouldn't be flattering. I'm not stupid enough to get that close to a girl like her."

"But—"

"No buts, Sunshine." He glanced back over his shoulder where Dane held Lis's attention. "That girl is shallow and rude. She's a horrible friend and probably the worst girlfriend on the planet. But the moment you walked around that bar with your little notebook and your 'hey, can I kiss you' line, I've been planning this."

Now I was just plain lost. But *planning* sounded nefarious.

"Planning what?" As soon as the words left my lips, I wanted them back. Never, ever, ever, ever-ever-evereverevereverever ask a question you don't want the answer to.

"Did you know you hum constantly? You sing under your breath even when there's not music." He took another step toward me, but the wall held off my retreat. "You bop around in that head of yours watching everything and staying out of the way. You let her be the center of attention when she can't hold a candle to you. She's dull and self-centered."

I glanced past him. I knew it was all true—well, the part about letting her be the center of attention. Earlier in the evening I'd begun to really see what type of friend I had in her. The worst thing she could have done for our friendship was drag me out tonight. I was a great lunch-on-Sunday friend for her, but seeing the way she was...the way she expected me to be...I'd already known in the back of my heart that she wasn't going to be anywhere near my inner circle after this.

"I thought, if I could get you out, get you into the spotlight, you'd shine." His grin hitched up. "And you did. When you sang, everyone stopped. They couldn't help themselves. But the second you handed that microphone back, she took over again."

He was right. And I knew what he wasn't saying...I *let* her take it back.

"I don't know how to be like her."

His head tilted to the side, the smile shifting again, getting softer, kinder.

"You don't have to be like her. That's the whole point. No guy in his right mind would really be interested in her." He hitched his thumb back in their direction. "She's a puddle."

He was so close now, I could feel him as if we touched in all the places we didn't. It was daunting and exciting. It scared the snot out of me because I loved having him so near.

The street value of the Ben-drug in Jennaland would be off the charts.

He pulled my notebook out of his back pocket and all I could think was *who cares about the stupid notebook*. See? Ben-drug, addictive and dangerous.

He bopped me on the nose with my own property and then held it there between us.

"I thought you might want this back."

"Oh? You think?" Finally, Jenna. Join the conversation, for crying out loud. "No clue what gave you that idea."

I snatched the notebook out of his hand, ready to make my escape before I made a huge fool of myself.

"Well, I figured you'd want to have it on you." His hand came up to brush across my cheek, pushing my loose hair out of my eyes. "You know. To take notes."

Before I knew what he meant to do, or could argue with him about the pity kiss, his lips brushed mine. And then they took mine. And then I lost track of time...maybe even days...or years.

It wasn't so much that it made me remember past kisses. It was more like it made me forget every other kiss I'd ever had.

He lifted himself away and then set his forehead against mine.

"So, you ready to make our escape? Dane's covering for us and I know a great place that serves crepes all night."

Wait. That sounded suspiciously like a date.

"It is a date, Sunshine."

Oh for crazy-girl-talking-out-loud sake.

He wrapped his hand around my free one and nodded toward my notebook. "I'm hoping you're looking for more than just first kiss research. Second kisses can be really difficult to remember too."

And I was hoping he was thinking about second date notes.

"I am."

Geez.

~*~

Thanks so much for reading *The Last Single Girl* and *It's in His Kiss*. I've had so much fun writing stories in The Brew. I hope they gave you a little bit of love, laughter, and friendship in your day.

Want More of Jenna, Ben & Their Friends?
THE BREW HA HA SERIES

It's in His Kiss
The Last Single Girl
Worth The Fall
The Catching Kind

BREW AFTER DARK Shorts
Love in Tune
Sweet as Cake

~*~

YA Books by Bria Quilnan

Secret Girlfriend (RVHS #1)
Secret Life (RVHS #2)
Wreckless

~~*~~

Bria Quinlan writes sweet and sassy rom coms because if you can't laugh in love...when can you? Check out her non-story ramblings www.caitiequinn.com.

~~*~~

65903901R00095

Made in the USA
San Bernardino, CA
07 January 2018